# RUMP

# RUMP

### THE (FAIRLY) TRUE TALE OF
## RUMPELSTILTSKIN

## LIESL SHURTLIFF

A YEARLING BOOK

This is a work of fiction. Names, characters, places, and incidents either are the product of the author's imagination or are used fictitiously. Any resemblance to actual persons, living or dead, events, or locales is entirely coincidental.

Text copyright © 2013 by Liesl Shurtliff
Cover art copyright © 2018 by Kevin Keele
Title type copyright © 2018 by Jacey

All rights reserved. Published in the United States by Yearling, an imprint of Random House Children's Books, a division of Penguin Random House LLC, New York. Originally published under the title *Rump: The True Story of Rumpelstiltskin* in hardcover in the United States by Alfred A. Knopf, an imprint of Random House Children's Books, New York, in 2013.

Yearling and the jumping horse design are registered trademarks of Penguin Random House LLC.

Visit us on the Web! rhcbooks.com

Educators and librarians, for a variety of teaching tools, visit us at RHTeachersLibrarians.com

The Library of Congress has cataloged the hardcover edition of this work as follows:
Shurtliff, Liesl.
Rump : the true story of Rumpelstiltskin / Liesl Shurtliff. — 1st ed.
p. cm.
Summary: Relates the tale of Rumpelstiltskin's childhood and youth, explaining why his name is so important, how he is able to spin straw into gold, and why a first-born child is his reward for helping the miller's daughter-turned-queen.
ISBN 978-0-307-97793-9 (trade) — ISBN 978-0-307-97794-6 (lib. bdg.) —
ISBN 978-0-307-97795-3 (ebook)
[1. Fairy tales. 2. Names, Personal—Fiction. 3. Magic—Fiction. 4. Gold—Fiction.
5. Humorous stories.] I. Title.
PZ8.S34525 Rum 2013 [Fic]—dc23 2012005093
ISBN 978-0-307-97796-0 (pbk.)

Printed in the United States of America
20 19

Random House Children's Books supports the First Amendment and celebrates the right to read.

FOR Scott,
my best friend in the whole world

# CONTENTS

# CHAPTER ONE

## Your Name Is Your Destiny

My mother named me after a cow's rear end. It's the favorite village joke, and probably the only one, but it's not really true. At least I don't think it's true, and neither does Gran. Really, my mother had another name for me, a wonderful name, but no one ever heard it. They only heard the first part. The worst part.

Mother had been very ill when I was born. Gran said she was fevered and coughing and I came before I was supposed to. Still, my mother held me close and whispered my name in my ear. No one heard it but me.

"His name?" Gran asked. "Tell me his name."

"His name is Rump . . . *haaa-cough-cough-cough* . . ." Gran gave Mother something warm to drink and pried me from her arms.

"Tell me his name, Anna. All of it."

But Mother never did. She took a breath and then let out all the air and didn't take any more in. Ever.

Gran said that I cried then, but I never hear that in my imagination. All I hear is silence. Not a move or a breath. The fire doesn't crack and even the pixies are still.

Finally, Gran holds me up and says, "Rump. His name is Rump."

The next morning, the village bell chimed and gnomes ran all over The Mountain crying, "Rump! Rump! The new boy's name is Rump!"

My name couldn't be changed or taken back, because in The Kingdom your name isn't just what people call you. Your name is full of meaning and power. Your name is your destiny.

My destiny really stinks.

I stopped growing when I was eight and I was small to begin with. The midwife, Gertrude, says I'm small because I had only the milk of a weak goat instead of a strong mother, but I know that really it's because of my name. You can't grow all the way if you don't have a whole name.

I tried not to think about my destiny too much, but on my birthday I always did. On my twelfth birthday I thought of nothing else. I sat in the mine, swirling mud around in a pan, searching for gold. We needed gold, gold, gold, but all I saw was mud, mud, mud.

The pickaxes beat out a rhythm that rang all over The Mountain. It filled the air with thumps and bumps. In my head The Mountain was chanting, *Thump, thump, thump. Bump, bump, bump. Rump, Rump, Rump.* At least it was a good rhyme.

> *Thump, thump, thump*
> *Bump, bump, bump*
> *Rump, Rump, Rump*

"Butt! Hey, Butt!"

I groaned as Frederick and his brother Bruno approached with menacing grins on their faces. Frederick and Bruno were the miller's sons. They were close to my age, but so big, twice my size and ugly as trolls.

"Happy birthday, Butt! We have a present just for you." Frederick threw a clod of dirt at me. My stubby hands tried to block it, but it smashed right in my face and I gagged at the smell. The clod of dirt was not dirt.

"Now that's a gift worthy of your name!" said Bruno.

Other children howled with laughter.

"Leave him alone," said a girl named Red. She glared at Frederick and Bruno, holding her shovel over her shoulder like a weapon. The other children stopped laughing.

"Oh," said Frederick. "Do you love Butt?"

"That's not his name," growled Red.

"Then what is it? Why doesn't he tell us?"

"Rump!" I said without thinking. "My name is Rump!" They burst out laughing. I had done just what they wanted. "But that's not my real name!" I said desperately.

"It isn't?" asked Frederick.

"What do you think his real name is?" asked Bruno.

Frederick pretended to think very hard. "Something unusual. Something special . . . Cow Rump."

"Baby Rump," said Bruno.

"Rump Roast!"

Everyone laughed. Frederick and Bruno fell over each other, holding their stomachs while tears streamed down their faces. They rolled in the dirt and squealed like pigs.

Just for a moment I envied them. They looked like they were having such fun, rolling in the dirt and laughing. Why couldn't I do that? Why couldn't I join them?

Then I remembered why they were laughing.

Red swung her shovel down hard so it stuck in the ground right between the boys' heads. Frederick and Bruno stopped laughing. "Go away," she said.

Bruno swallowed, staring cross-eyed at the shovel that was just inches from his nose. Frederick stood and grinned at Red. "Sure. You two want to be alone." The brothers walked away, snorting and falling over each other.

I could feel Red looking at me, but I stared down at my pan. I picked out some of Frederick and Bruno's present. I did not want to look at Red.

"You'd better find some gold today, Rump," said Red.

I glared at her. "I know. I'm not *stupid*."

She raised her eyebrows. Some people did think I was stupid because of my name. And sometimes I thought they were probably right. Maybe if you have only half a name, you have only half a brain.

I kept my eyes on my pan of mud, hoping Red would go away, but she stood over me with her shovel, like she was inspecting me.

"The rations are tightening," said Red. "The king—"

"I *know*, Red."

Red glared at me. "Fine. Then good luck to you." She stomped off, and I felt worse than when Frederick and Bruno threw poop in my face.

Red wasn't my friend exactly, but she was the closest I had to a friend. She never made fun of me. Sometimes she stood up for me, and I understood why. Her name wasn't all that great, either. Just as people laugh at a name like *Rump*, they fear a name like *Red*. *Red* is not a name. It's a color, an *evil* color. What kind of destiny does that bring?

I swirled mud in my pan, searching for a glimmer. Our village lives off The Mountain's gold—what little there is to find. The royal tax collector gathers it and takes it to the king. King Barf. If King Barf is pleased with our gold, he sends us extra food for rations. If he's not pleased, we are extra hungry.

King Barf isn't actually named King Barf. His real name is King Bartholomew Archibald Reginald Fife, a fine, kingly name—a name with a great destiny, of course. But I don't care how handsome or powerful that name makes you. It's a mouthful. So for short I call him King Barf, though I'd never say it out loud.

A pixie flew in my face, a blur of pink hair and translucent wings. I held still as she landed on my arm and explored. I tried to gently shake her off, but she only fluttered her wings and continued her search. She was looking for gold, just like me.

Pixies are obsessed with gold. Once, they had been very helpful in the mines since they can sense large veins of gold from a mile away and deep in the earth. Whenever a swarm of pixies would hover around a particular spot of rock, the miners knew precisely where they should dig.

But there hasn't been much gold in The Mountain for many years. We find only small pebbles and specks. The pixies don't dance and chirp the way they used to. Now they're just pests, pesky thieves trying to steal what little gold we find. And they'll bite you to get it. Pixies are no bigger than a finger and they look sweet and delicate and harmless with their sparkly wings and colorful hair, but their bites hurt worse than bee stings and squirrel bites and poison ivy combined—and I've had them all.

The pixie on my arm finally decided I had no gold and flew away. I scooped more mud from the sluice and swirled it around in my pan. No gold. Only mud, mud, mud.

*Thump, thump, thump*
*Bump, bump, bump*
*Rump, Rump, Rump*

I didn't find any gold. We worked until the sun was low and a gnome came running through the mines shouting, "The day is done! The day is done!" in a voice so bright and cheery I had the urge to kick the gnome and send it flying down The Mountain. But I was relieved. Now I could go home, and maybe Gran had cooked a chicken. Maybe she would tell me a story that would help me stop thinking about my birth and name and destiny.

I set my tools aside and walked alone down The

Mountain and through The Village. Red walked alone too, a little ahead of me. The rest of the villagers traveled in clusters, some children together, others with their parents. Some carried leather purses full of gold. Those who found good amounts of gold got extra rations. If they found a great deal, they could keep some to trade in the markets. I had never found enough gold even for extra rations.

Pixies fluttered in front of my face and chirped in my ears, and I swatted at them. If only the pixies would show me a mound of gold in the earth, then maybe it wouldn't matter that I was small. If I found lots of gold, then maybe no one would laugh at me or make fun of my name. Gold would make me worth something.

# CHAPTER TWO

## Spinning Wheels and Pixie Thrills

> *Home is a place to get out of the rain*
> *It cradles the hurt and mends the pain*
> *And no one cares about your name*
> *Or the height of your head*
> *Or the size of your brain*

I made up that rhyme myself.

Rhymes make me feel better when I'm down. The midwife, Gertrude, told me that rhymes are a waste of brain space, but I like the way they sound. When you say the words and the sounds match, it feels like everything in the world is in its place and whatever you say is powerful and true.

My home is a tiny cottage. The roof is lopsided and leaks when it rains, but Gran is there and she doesn't care about my name.

When I stepped inside, I was greeted by a gust of warm air that smelled of bread and onions. Gran was sewing near the fire and didn't stop her work when I entered, but greeted me with a smile and a rhyme.

"Wash your hands, wipe your feet, give me a kiss, sit down and eat."

Gran's rhyme made my insides warm. She didn't mention my birthday, and I felt light again. I obeyed all of Gran's instructions and sat on the woven rug by the fire. I ladled some onion soup into a bowl and sipped.

"Tell me what your day was about," said Gran.

I wouldn't tell her about Frederick and Bruno's gift. It would either make her very sad or very mad, and I hated to see Gran upset. I decided to turn the subject to the least awful thing about the day.

"I didn't find any gold," I said.

"Humph," said Gran. "Nothing to be ashamed of. Not much gold left in The Mountain. Eat your supper."

There were two thin slices of bread sitting on the hearth. I swallowed one in two gulps and eyed the other.

"Eat it," said Gran.

"What about you?"

"I already ate. Stuffed as gooseberry pie." I looked at Gran's frail and withered frame. Her hands were knobby and the blue veins were raised above her skin. She trembled as she tried to feed thread into a needle. I knew she wasn't eating enough, that she was going hungry to give me more food. Me, a boy who hadn't grown in years.

"I'm not hungry," I said.

"Fine, then, take it to the chickens," she said.

I stared at the bread. I was so hungry. Not hungry enough to steal food from my gran, but hungry enough to steal food from the chickens. I took the bread and ate it, but it didn't fill me.

I was twelve now. Twelve was the age most boys were considered men and they started working in the tunnels with pickaxes, searching for big gold. I wasn't even allowed to pick up a shovel. With my half of a name, I was half of a person.

Sometimes I thought if I just focused hard enough, I could remember the name my mother had whispered to me before she died. Sometimes I could still hear that whisper in my ear. Rump . . . Rumpus, Rumpalini, Rumpalicious, Rumperdink, Rumpty-dumpty. I had spoken a hundred names aloud. It always tickled my brain like a feather, but my true name, if I really had one, never surfaced all the way.

"Gran, what if I never find my name?"

Gran's needle paused in the air for a moment. "You mustn't worry about it too much, dear."

That's what she always said if I asked about my name or my destiny. I used to think she just wanted me to be patient and not worry. I thought she was reassuring me that all would work out well, that someday I would find my name and have a great destiny. But now I realized that maybe she said it because I might never find my real name.

"Suppose I'm Rump until the day I die?" I said.

"You're young yet," said Gran. "Rump might turn out

to be a great destiny . . . in the *end*." I saw her bite her cheeks to keep in a laugh.

"It's not funny, Gran," I said, though I was stifling my own laughter. Life would be awfully grim and glum if I couldn't laugh at myself.

"Everyone is born and everyone dies," said Gran. "And if you're Rump until the day you die, I'll love you just the same."

"But what about the in-between?" I said. "It's all the things in the middle that make a person special. How can I live a special life without a special name?"

"You can start by fetching me some firewood," said Gran. This was her way of telling me to stop feeling sorry for myself. Life goes on. Get to work.

I stepped out the back of our cottage and took a deep breath of crisp air. Summer was fading. The leaves on the trees were turning from green to yellow. Milk, our goat, stood tethered to a tree, chewing leaves off a shrub.

"Hello, Milk," I said. Milk bleated a greeting.

Our donkey, Nothing, wasn't tied up or penned in because he wouldn't move unless his tail was on fire. "Hello, Nothing," I said. Nothing said nothing.

We don't name animals. Names are special and saved for people, but I feel like I need to call them something, so I call our goat Milk, because that's what she gives us, and I call our donkey Nothing, because that's what he's good for. He used to help my father in the mines, but I can't get him to do a thing. So he's Nothing, and his name makes me feel a little better about my own.

I gathered wood in my arms, and the chickens pecked around my feet for the bugs that dropped from the logs. The woodpile was getting low. I was thinking how I would need to get more from the woodcutter soon when something caught my eye. An odd-shaped piece of wood was sticking above the pile. It was curved and smooth. I pushed some logs away and saw spokes and spindles. It was a spinning wheel. I paused, confused. Spinning wheels in The Mountain were rare. I only knew what one looked like because the miller's daughter had a spinning wheel and she would spin people's wool for some extra gold or some of their rations. Sometimes that was cheaper than trading for cloth and yarn in the markets. But I'd never seen anyone else with one. What was a spinning wheel doing in the woodpile?

After I placed the wood by the hearth, I asked Gran about the wheel. She waved me away and stayed focused on her sewing. "Oh, that old thing. It's rubbish. We might as well use it for firewood."

"Where did it come from?" I asked.

"It belonged to your mother."

Mother's spinning wheel! Just knowing it was hers and she had spun on it made me feel like I knew her better. "Do you have anything she spun?"

"No," said Gran in a tight voice. "She sold everything she spun."

"May I have the spinning wheel?" I asked.

"It's probably too warped to be useful. It would serve us better in the fire."

"I don't have anything from my mother. She would've wanted me to have something of hers."

"Not that."

"Please, Gran. Let me have it. For my birthday." Gran finally looked up at me. I never talked about my birthday, but I wanted the spinning wheel. It was like a tiny part of my mother, and if we burned it, she would go away forever.

Gran sighed. "You keep it out of my way. I don't want to trip over it."

I worked through the last bit of daylight and into the dark, moving the woodpile so I could get to the wheel. I brought it inside and placed it next to my bed. I brushed my hands over the scratched and warped wood as if it were the finest gold. I spun the wheel and was surprised it didn't wobble or creak. It made a soft whirring sound, almost musical. A few pixies came out from the cracks and danced upon it, chirping in their tiny voices. Gran scowled. She looked at the wheel as if it were a pile of mud all over her floor.

"Can I try it?" I asked eagerly.

"You're too small," said Gran. "When you're a little bigger perhaps."

I frowned. I hadn't grown in four years. "I can stretch my legs, see? And we have some wool. . . ."

"No," said Gran sharply, then she softened. "It's a messy business, dear, even if you know how, and I wouldn't want you to get your fingers caught."

"Maybe the miller's daughter—"

"Use some sense, child," Gran cut me off sharply. "She'll think you're trying to steal business from her, and the miller will probably withhold our rations, the lying cheat." Gran was red in the face. I stepped back a little as she took a deep breath.

"Your father meant to chop it to firewood, anyway. Your mother didn't like to spin. She hated it. Only spun because . . . she had to." Gran closed her eyes and sighed, as if talking about my parents took great amounts of energy. She never spoke of my mother or father. My father had been her only child, and he died in the mines before I was born. It must have been painful for Gran to think about. And she never spoke of my mother, I guessed because she knew so little of her. Only now I suspected Gran knew more than she let on, but for some reason, she wanted to keep it from me.

Late at night, when the fire was only a few glowing coals and Gran was snoring, I slipped out of bed and sat at the spinning wheel. I placed my hands on the wood. Even in the dim light, I could see that it was old, warped and scratched from years of rain and snow and heat. But, still, it was like a silent companion, just biding its time until it could speak to me, until we could speak to each other.

*There's wool in the cupboard,* said a small voice in my head. *Gran will never know.*

The voice was very persuasive and I was easy to persuade. I fetched the wool.

I had to stretch to reach the treadle. My foot made jerky motions as it pushed down, but soon the wheel spun with a familiar rhythm, like a song sung to me in the cradle.

*Whir, whir, whir.*

My heart raced with the music, the swells and beats of the spinning making me large and full of life.

I fed some wool into the wheel, but my fingers got caught and it came to a harsh halt, pinching my hand in the spokes. I yanked my hand away, feeling the skin tear as I fell back onto the floor.

A few pixies emerged from cracks in the fireplace and flew over to the wheel. I sat still, cradling my injured finger. More pixies fluttered around the spinning wheel, dancing on the spindle and the spokes. Then they came to me. They crawled up my neck and pranced on my head and giggled. Pixie voices are so high and shrill that their giggles ring in your ears. The buzzards drove me insane. The only thing I appreciated about pixies was that their very existence gave me hope that there was still gold in The Mountain. But why were they pestering me now, when I wasn't near any gold?

A pixie landed on my nose, tickling it. I sneezed and the pixies squealed and shot away for a moment but then came back, full of squeaky chatter.

A pixie with bright red hair and leaflike wings landed on my bleeding fingers and dug her tiny feet into my cut. It felt like the stab of a fat needle. I let out a cry of pain and then bit down on my tongue.

Gran stopped snoring.

The pixies scooped up the bits of wool around the wheel, laughing their tinkly giggles, and flew up the chimney.

Silently, I slipped into bed and wrapped my bleeding

finger in the blankets. I heard Gran slowly walk toward me. I closed my eyes and tried to breathe deep. After a minute of silence, I peeked and saw her staring at the wheel.

"Foolishness," she said. "More useful in the fire." She gripped the wheel and pulled it so it scraped along the floor. My heart pounded. I thought she really would put it in the fire, but she let it go and went back to bed. Soon she was snoring again.

My heart raced for a long time. My finger throbbed. I felt like the spinning wheel had bitten me, like it had clamped down on me because it didn't want me to spin. But the pixies had been dancing around me as if they *did* want me to spin. I wasn't sure which I should listen to, the pixies or the wheel.

# CHAPTER THREE

## The Greedy Miller and His Daughter

I woke as the village bell chimed for the mining day to begin. Gran was still sleeping, so I took some dry bread and a little goat cheese and walked outside.

Pixies instantly flew at me, chirping and screeching. I staggered and swatted at them. Then I stepped in Nothing's poop.

Such is my destiny.

A gnome ran right in front of me and nearly knocked me off my feet. He chanted, "Message for Bertrand, message for Bertrand," over and over. He wouldn't stop until he found Bertrand.

Gnomes are very useful in The Kingdom, especially in The Village, where most people can't read any letters. Gran made me learn some, but gnomes love to spread news and deliver messages. They have some kind of sense that lets them know when they've reached the right person, and they won't stop until they do.

More gnomes were emerging from their holes in the ground, eager to gather messages and deliver them to the rightful recipients. Gnomes had little holes all over The Village, in the middle of roads, between the roots of trees, and on the edges of rocks. They looked just like rabbit holes, but supposedly gnome holes all led to a large underground cavern where they kept hoards of food. That's what we all guessed, since gnomes are quite chubby but you never see them eating above the ground. Frederick and Bruno once tried to dig down to their hoard but gave up after they dug twelve feet and still couldn't see a thing.

The mines were a nightmare that day. My finger throbbed and so did my head. Frederick and Bruno thought it hilarious to throw pebbles at my head every time they brought dirt to the sluices. The pixies pestered me all day. I hoped it was a sign that great amounts of gold were in the mud, but I didn't find any.

When the mining day was done, everyone walked together toward the mill. Today was rations day. I walked behind Red while my stomach grumbled with each footstep, the chant of *food, food, food.*

When we arrived at the mill, there was lots of shouting. Old Rupert was shaking his fist in the miller's face.

"You're a filthy liar, you cheat! Sacks of gold I've mined! I've earned ten times as much grain as this!" Old Rupert hollered. Rupert was a rickety old man, barely able to walk; yet he still worked with a pickax in the mines.

"Upon the honor of my name, good Rupert," the

miller said in his oily voice, "I've given what is fairly yours. It always seems less after the grinding."

"Hogwash! I find lots of gold, and look! You call this fair?" Rupert shook the flour sack at the miller and then turned around and shook it at all the villagers. There couldn't have been enough flour to bake two loaves of bread.

"Times are hard," said the miller. "We all must tighten the belt." He laughed and his big belly laughed with him. Such a good joke for a fat miller with ten plump children!

"You dirty cheat! Rotten swindler!"

"Now, Rupert," said the miller with a bit of warning, "that kind of ingratitude won't work in your favor. Suppose next week there weren't any rations for you at all?" Rupert went silent. Finally, he hobbled away down the road, muttering curses loudly enough for all to hear.

The next woman took her meager rations without a word, and the rest of the villagers did too.

Gran always says that the miller, Oswald, is a cheat. The royal tax collector doesn't like to come to The Mountain any more than he has to, so he simply sends up carts full of food and supplies and gives Oswald charge of all the rations from our gold to distribute as he sees fit. Gran says Oswald always takes more than his fair share. But what could we do? We weren't mining much gold lately, and we didn't really know how much food was stored. Only Oswald did, and Oswald decided how much food we had earned for our work. The whole village was hungry, except the miller and his family. Could a name make you greedy like mine made me small?

As I drew closer to the front of the line, a whirling motion caught my eye. The miller's daughter, Opal, was spinning outside on the porch. I watched, transfixed. I studied how her foot pushed on the treadle and how her hands rhythmically fed the wool. The wool thinned and tightened and transformed into yarn, as if by magic.

"You enjoy the spinning, do you?" The miller was right in front of me now, and everyone else had gone. How long had I been staring at Opal?

"I'm just curious how it works," I said.

The miller lifted his bushy eyebrows. "Spinning's a woman's work, but she could show you . . . for a price." He lifted two bags of food, our rations. I wanted to say yes. Something inside of me ached to spin. My foot twitched with the rhythm of Opal's spinning. My fingers itched to feed one thing through the wheel and watch it transform to another before my very eyes. I almost said yes, and then I thought of Gran. I could starve myself for weeks to learn the spinning, but I couldn't betray Gran.

"Oh," I said. "No. I just like to watch."

"Yes," said the miller. "My Opal is the jewel of The Mountain. She will marry well."

My face heated. I wasn't talking about *her*. Why would *I* look at her like *that*?

Sure, she was pretty, with her golden hair and ruby lips. Hans Jacob had offered the miller four sheep and a milking cow for her hand in marriage. It was a fortune! But the miller flatly refused. Opal was worth much more than that, he said. Hans Jacob left with his head low, and everyone thought the miller was crazy. Did he expect a royal marriage?

Just at that moment, Opal looked up at me. I noticed something I hadn't before. She was beautiful, yes, but her face looked sort of blank. Opal stared at me and then flicked out her tongue and wound it around her mouth, like a frog catching flies. Not so beautiful. She did it again, a kind of nervous tic. I wondered if Hans Jacob had noticed these things. Maybe they would make him feel better.

The miller placed my rations at my feet. "Find a little extra gold and I'll have Opal show you how to spin. She is a fine spinner, but I've known some who possess a more . . . natural talent." He looked down at me with a strange smile on his face. Was he being kind? I'd never known the miller to be kind.

I took the rations home, but Gran was resting, so there was nothing to eat but a bit of cheese. I fed Milk and Nothing and the chickens, and they all bleated and brayed and clucked at me for more. A pixie flew in my face and a gnome ran under my feet chanting, "Message for Gertrude! Message for Gertrude!" in an urgent voice. Another baby probably.

Suddenly the world felt crowded and noisy. I didn't want to be around anyone or anything. I just wanted to be alone. And there's only one place on The Mountain where you can count on being alone. The Woods.

Most people avoid The Woods because of the trolls and ogres. It's also home to The Witch of The Woods, and witches are best left alone. I heard of a witch who liked to catch children and cook them for her supper! And Gran told me of a witch who stole a baby right from her parents' arms and locked her in a tower where she could never get out. What a horrible thing to steal a baby!

But the biggest danger of a witch was her magic. There was no telling what terrors a witch could manage—brew a storm right over your head, or turn you into a fat pig to eat you for dinner. Skinny as I was, I didn't want to take any chances, so I didn't go far—just far enough to be surrounded by tall trees where no one from The Village would see me. Here and there were tree stumps from the woodcutter. He was the only person who ever went deep into The Woods. I sat on one of the stumps.

Through the trees I could see out over the valley where The Kingdom lay. The houses looked so tiny I could cover them with my thumb. Beyond the houses was the king's castle. That took both my hands to cover. After that there was nothing but roads that led to the villages Yonder and Beyond.

Just as we don't name our animals, we don't name the places where we live. We simply call them what they are or where they are—The Mountain, The Kingdom, Yonder. . . . I think it's boring, but I guess we put so much thought and energy into naming babies, we don't have any left over.

A pixie landed on my hand and I swatted it away. It squeaked and chirped and flew at me again.

This pixie had blue hair and large, glassy wings. He

looked so sweet and harmless that I forgot sense and stuck my finger out to him, as if he were a tame bird. He landed on me and giggled. He had such a smug and teasing look on his face, like he knew a secret about me. Maybe he knew where all the gold was buried.

Two more pixies landed on me. I brushed them off, gently. They darted away but then came back. One landed on my shoulder, another on my ear, then another and another. They danced on my head, my arms, my fingers, squealing and chirping. I tried to shake them off until I lost my balance and fell off the tree stump.

Then the pixies attacked. They shot at me like an explosion of many-colored sparks. One bit my arm. More bit my hands. I kicked and thrashed to get them off.

"Buzzards!" I screamed, but they shrieked and converged on me like a flying army. Another one bit my neck.

Then something showered down on top of me, and when I opened my mouth to yell, I got a mouthful of dirt. More dirt came down. It was raining dirt. The pixies shrieked louder than ever and flew away in a swarm. When I got the dirt out of my eyes, they had disappeared and I looked up to see a girl.

It was Red.

She stared at me all curious and said, "Are you made of gold or something?"

# CHAPTER FOUR

## Red and Her Grandmother

I lay on the ground, still as a dead chicken, and looked up at Red.

"Pixies don't attack like that unless your pockets are full of gold," said Red. "Did you steal some?"

"No," I said, scrambling to my feet. I brushed off the dirt and backed away a little. Even though Red never made fun of me, she still made me nervous. Once, a boy teased Red about her name and she punched him in the nose so hard her name was running down his face. That's when everyone understood *her* destiny.

"I'm not going to hit you," she said, as if she could read my mind. "What are you doing in The Woods?"

"Just thinking," I said. I wanted to ask her the same question, but suddenly Red stepped forward and pointed to my neck.

"They bit you," she said with a suspicious glare. "Pixies

don't bug you unless you're near gold. They definitely don't bite unless you *have* gold. Lots of it."

Suddenly I became aware of the throbbing pain all over me. Four of my fingers looked like sausages. A big lump was growing out of my arm, and my shirt collar tightened around my swelling neck. Red was right. I'd never known a pixie to bite unless you were holding a big chunk of gold. But I didn't have any. I turned out my pockets and held out my hands to show Red. "How did you get rid of the pixies?" I asked.

She held up her fists and dropped the dirt in them. "Pixies hate to be dirty. They like to stay shiny."

I would keep a pot of dirt by my bed and by the fireplace. With the way they just attacked me, maybe I would carry a bag of dirt with me everywhere.

The village bell began to chime, making us both jump.

"Baby's been born," said Red.

"Yes," I said.

Soon a gnome would run throughout the village announcing the baby's name. After the name was spread, the villagers would talk all day about the quality of the name, the length, and the sounds. They'd discuss what kind of destiny the name would bestow upon the child.

"I hate that bell," said Red.

"Me too."

"And I hate gnomes."

"Me too." In my head I always imagined the bell ringing and the gnomes shouting, "Rump! Rump! The new boy's name is Rump!" I wondered if Red had those same thoughts about her name. Even though it wasn't embarrassing, it made her different. Maybe we were both lonely because of our names.

"Why do we just name babies?" I suddenly asked.

"What do you mean?"

"Why don't we give a name to The Mountain, or The Kingdom, or roads or animals, or even The Woods?"

Red looked at me funny. "Those things don't need names," she said. "Everybody knows that. Names hold power, and that power shouldn't be wasted on something that isn't living. A village doesn't need a destiny."

"But sometimes places *feel* alive. Sometimes they feel powerful, like they *could* have a destiny, just like people. Like these trees. They feel alive."

"They *are* alive," said Red, "but that doesn't mean they need a name. They don't have a destiny like we do."

"Well, what about The Village? Wouldn't it be nice to give our village a good name, like . . . Asteria or Ochenleff? That way, if you wanted to go on an adventure, you could say, 'I'm leaving Asteria at last!' Or if you were coming home, you could say, 'Ah. Ochenleff, my home.' It would be like greeting a long-lost friend, instead of a mountain full of metal, or just dirt. And maybe it *would* have a destiny then."

"That's the craziest thing I ever heard," said Red, but she was also smiling.

We heard the gnomes in the distance, shouting something in their gravelly little voices. Finally, a gnome ran right past us. "Furball! The name of the new daughter is Furball! Furball!"

Red and I stared at each other. Then we burst out

laughing. We laughed and laughed and curled over our stomachs. We laughed until tears were streaming from our eyes, but then something appeared from the darkness of the trees and loomed over Red.

I stopped laughing. Red still giggled until a thin, knobby hand touched her shoulder. Red looked up and squealed.

"Granny!" She looked around nervously, as if to see who else was watching. "W-w-what are you doing here?"

"I'll go where I please, girl." Her voice was remarkably steady, even though she looked ancient. Her cheeks sagged past her jaw and she was hunched over on a gnarled stick that shook under her hand.

"But—"

"Hold your but! What's so hilarious?"

"Nothing," said Red. She nudged me while keeping wide eyes on her granny.

"Nothing at all," my voice squeaked.

Red's granny squinted at me. "You're Elsbith's boy."

"I'm her grandson."

"Well, how is she? A crabby old wretch still, no doubt."

"Yes, ma'am. I mean no, ma'am, she's fine."

"You're the one with only half your name."

I shuffled my feet and glanced at Red.

"Oh, stop your worry prancing. Red already knows. She won't tell."

How did they know? Gran had told me never to tell anyone that *Rump* wasn't my whole name. Some people might think a half name would make a person addled in the brain or even dangerous.

Red's granny leaned down close to me. She had a strong, but not unpleasant smell, like fresh things that grow in the earth. "Hmm . . . ," she said, staring into my eyes. "You'll find it all."

"What all?"

"Your name. All of it."

"I will?" Red's granny suddenly looked very wise and maybe even less crouched and wrinkly.

"Not before you cause a heap of trouble, though. And you have to find your destiny first."

"But I thought my name was my destiny."

"No, no, other way around. Find your destiny, you find your name. It's right under your feet." I looked under my feet. Just dirt.

My brain felt all tangled. Red's granny came even closer and hunched over so her face was level with mine. It felt like she was looking through me and around me and beyond me all at once. "One more thing." She pointed her gnarled finger at me. "Watch your step."

"What step?"

The old woman ignored my question and looked between Red and me. "And just what were you two hee-hawing about?"

"Nothing," Red and I insisted for the second time.

"Oh, it's not nothing. That new baby's name is funny to you, isn't it? Well, I wouldn't think either of you would have the right to laugh at such a name."

"Don't we have more right than anyone?" I asked. "Ouch!" Red dug her heel into my foot, but her granny's mouth twitched into half a smile.

"For someone with half a name, you're pretty smart," said Red's granny. "Give Elsbith my warm regards, crabby old wretch."

I stared after the old woman as she hobbled away and disappeared in the trees.

"Your granny's strange."

Red turned red all over and stamped her heel on my other foot. "She is not." She marched off, kicking up dirt that flew in my face.

At least I was safe from another pixie attack.

At home, I told Gran that Red's granny sent her warm regards, but left out the "crabby old wretch" part. "Hmph," said Gran. "Crabby old wretch." Maybe all old women think that about each other.

I lay awake that night for a long time. The old woman's words kept poking at my brain, refusing to let me sleep. She said I would find all of my name. How? I forgot to ask her how. Then she said I would cause a lot of trouble. How? She also told me to watch my step. Well, that was probably just general advice. I was always tripping.

But the words that kept running through my mind over and over were *Find your destiny, find your name.* Where? Where was it?

For some reason, I kept looking at the spinning wheel. It sat in a shaft of moonlight, still just biding its time. Waiting for me to spin.

# CHAPTER FIVE

## Fluff to Mouse, Mouse to Mice

The next rations day, Red and I walked home together from the mill. We hugged our rations sacks to us, the promise of fresh bread inside them. I wanted to ask Red more about her granny and the things she had said to me, but I didn't dare, not with the way she'd reacted when I said her granny was strange. Sometimes little things could make Red steaming mad. I just couldn't tell what those little things might be. That's the danger with Red. Unpredictable.

Suddenly Red groaned, and I looked up to see a tall, skinny man leaning against a tree, a giant sack flung over his shoulder.

"Kessler the peddler!" I shouted.

The man turned toward me, flipped his hat off his head, and bowed. His bright orange hair stuck out in every direction. Kessler was the only person we ever saw from The Kingdom besides the tax collector. He came to The Mountain to sell goods from The Kingdom—colorful threads, clay pots, and wooden spoons. Sometimes he had gold (likely from our mines) molded into rings and bracelets and chains. How funny that we dug up all that gold, but we could never afford to buy it back. But I wasn't interested in gold, and the thing I most wanted to see from Kessler wasn't in his old, patched-up sack.

"Children!" chimed Kessler. He looked around to see if we were alone, then whispered, "Come for a spell? An enchantment?"

Magic! I stepped forward, but Red grabbed my shirt collar and hauled me back. "Of course not," spat Red.

"Speak for yourself!" I shook her off. I had heard Frederick and Bruno talk of Kessler's magic. Nothing like a witch turning someone into a toad or making a storm, but he could touch fire, make things disappear, or turn one small thing into another. That's what I wanted most: to see him turn one thing into something else.

"Only cost you a scoop of grain," said Kessler.

I hesitated. Gran would be furious if she knew I'd traded even a tiny amount of our food for a magic trick. We had so little to begin with. Besides, she didn't approve of magic. I shook my head and stepped back.

"Oh, come, just *one* scoop. You won't starve for it. Bet you haven't had much fun in weeks, all that digging." Kessler gave a feeble smile. Suddenly I saw the hunger in his eyes, how hollow and sharp his cheeks were. He must be even hungrier than I was to sell a magic trick for a scoop of grain. Was I that hungry to see the magic?

"Can you turn one thing into another?"

"Of course, of course!" He waved me to come closer.

"Don't, Rump." I turned to see Red standing with her arms folded around her rations, glaring at Kessler.

Kessler frowned. "There's no harm in it."

"Says who?" asked Red. She suddenly looked very motherly. "Last time you came, you set Gus's hair on fire."

"Well, that was a bit of a—"

"And remember Helga and her wart—?"

"Purely coincidence!" said Kessler, cutting her off with a nervous laugh. He reached into his pockets. "Look, see? No fire, no warts. I will simply turn this bit of fuzz into . . . a mouse. A mouse!" He waved a tuft of lint in front of my face. Could he really turn it into a mouse? Gran told me a story of turning mice into horses and a pumpkin into a golden coach. Wouldn't it be fun to see a bit of fuzz turn into a live mouse?

"Rump," said Red through gritted teeth. "No." I ignored her. It was just a scoop of grain. Gran would hardly notice, and I'd skip breakfast in the morning. That was fair.

I opened my rations sack and Kessler whipped a tin cup from his pocket. He quickly scooped out a heap of flour and then pocketed it again. My stomach clenched. I'd have to skip three breakfasts for that. Red clucked her tongue in disappointment.

"And now," said Kessler, holding out the piece of lint, "I shall turn this little fuzz into a mouse!" Kessler cupped the fuzz in both hands and brought it close to his face. He muttered some words, and his eyes got big and glassy.

The fuzz started to tremble and swell. A tail poked out of one end, and the other end grew ears and a pointy little snout and made a tiny squeak. Last to take shape were four small paws and two beady black eyes.

A mouse! He had turned the fuzz into a mouse!

"Did you see?" I said to Red, pointing to the mouse.

"I saw," she said grumpily.

I smiled up at Kessler. He smiled back and put the mouse in his vest pocket. "Next time, maybe I'll turn the mouse into a cat!"

*Eep, eep!*

We looked down to see another mouse scurrying toward us. Then came another, and another. *Eep, eep! Eep!* Six mice were skittering over Kessler's feet. "Well, look at that!" He pulled the mouse out of his pocket. "They've come to greet their new friend! Isn't that magical?"

I started to nod in agreement, but then I heard strange noises, a pattering, like rain, and also a distant squeaking, like a flock of birds taking flight. The sounds got louder.

"Here it comes," said Red.

Kessler's eyes went wide. He held the mouse up and stared at it. "Oh. Oh, my—"

Then came the explosion. An explosion of mice! Hundreds of mice poured from trees and holes in the ground, through windows and under door cracks. Screams and shouts echoed throughout The Mountain. Something crashed in a nearby cottage, and a man threw open the door and fled with a dozen mice squeaking at his heels. The mice converged and ran toward us. I scrambled up a nearby tree and wrapped my legs around it.

"Time to go!" Kessler hitched up his pants, flung his sack over his shoulder, and ran, mice trailing in his wake.

Red laughed and shook her head. "That fool! He still hasn't learned to stay away from magic. He'd be safer playing with fire."

"But Kessler only does small tricks. What's wrong with that?"

"All magic has consequences, Rump. Even small magic can have big consequences."

"If he had turned it into a squirrel, would all the squirrels have attacked?"

"Something entirely different could have happened, something even worse. Like maybe he would have grown squirrel teeth." Red stuck out her teeth and wiggled her nose.

I laughed. Red dropped her squirrel face so she looked grave and grim. "For your food, Kessler takes the risk. But one day it will catch up to him. He might not even get to eat that food before the mice do."

I felt annoyed. What made her think she knew everything about magic? "Well, I thought it was brilliant. I should have paid him more," I said.

"Why?"

"He got rid of all the mice in The Village!"

Red stared at me, then shook her head and walked away.

If I could, I would do magic. I would change lots of things, for good, like make myself grow, or turn fuzz into food. I'd put more gold in The Mountain.

That bit of magic made me hungry for more. More magic, more transformation—and not from Kessler. I wanted magic all my own. How bad could the consequences be?

# CHAPTER SIX

## Gold! Gold! Gold!

That night I jerked awake to a shrill hum. A swarm of pixies hovered over me. One was on the tip of my nose, another on my ear, and two were walking down my chest. Several danced on my hands and chirped excitedly.

I held very still. I didn't want another attack like in The Woods. If only I had set a bucket of dirt by my bed. They tugged at my fingers, and with their combined efforts I felt an actual pull to get up.

It was still dark. Only a faint glow of moonlight spilled through the window, illuminating my bed and the spinning wheel. Across the room, Gran's snores were deep and even, undisturbed by the chattering and screeching of the pixies. Suddenly they were right in my ears, and their shrieks and chirps went straight to the center of my brain and shook in my skull. They were saying something. I had to strain to listen but they were chanting excitedly. I didn't know pixies could say real words.

"Gold! Gold! Gold!" it sounded like. The pixies tugged at my hair and ears and clothes. Dozens were wrapped around my fingers, furiously beating their wings in an effort to lift me from my bed. They were pulling me toward the spinning wheel.

And in that moment, an idea cracked open in my brain. It was like an egg had been sitting there quietly for a long time, and suddenly the egg hatched and out came the idea, and it was flying all around in my brain and would not stop flapping and chirping until it was let out. I had to let it out.

What if pixies couldn't just sense gold inside The Mountain? What if they could also sense it in a person, in someone who might possess the magic to take one thing—a piece of fluff or wool or straw—and turn it into . . .

"Gold! Gold! Gold!"

I rose from my bed and moved toward the spinning wheel. The pixies squeaked and flitted back and forth between me and the wheel. I placed my hands on the wheel and felt a vibration run through me. I spun it with my hand and listened to the whirring as if it had something to say that I needed to hear. Destiny. That's what this was.

I had no wool. The pixies had taken it all the last time I tried to spin. I looked around the cottage. There were chicken bones and chicken feathers and bits of yarn.

There were quilts and dishes and the big empty kettle in the hearth. I looked down at my feet. Destiny. *It's right under your feet.* Just dirt and . . . "Straw." I said it out loud.

"Gold! Gold! Gold!" the pixies sang in response.

I gathered the straw from the ground until I had a handful. I sat at the wheel. A few pixies fluttered around my hands and the straw and the bobbin.

"Gold! Gold! Gold!"

I fed the straw into the wheel.

*Whir, whir, whir.*

I spun the straw.

My breath caught in my chest. I stopped, unable to believe what I was seeing. In my hand were bits of straw, but around the bobbin were glowing, shimmering threads. I brushed my fingers over the threads, smooth and warm. *Gold.* I had just spun straw into gold.

I let my breath out and my whole chest swelled. Straw! More straw! I scrounged for more straw on the ground, all the little bits I could pick up. I fed them through the wheel. More gold! I ripped open my mattress and pulled out the straw. Who needed a straw mattress when you could sleep on gold?

I laughed and chanted rhymes as I spun.

> *One gold thread*
> *Will buy me bread*
> *A pile of thread*
> *Makes a crown for my head*

*Whir, whir, whir.*

I fed the straw into the wheel, rhythmically pulling and twisting it, and it made the most beautiful sound as it transformed into gold. A tinkling song, soft yet vibrant. More pixies burst from the crevices, and they all danced on the gold, twittering and screeching, "Gold, gold, gold!"

I laughed. I loved the pixies! I slid the silky gold off the bobbin and onto the floor to make room for more. I spun all the straw in my mattress. I spun until morning broke through the little window and sunlight made the gold glimmer. I stood and admired the fruits of my labor. A fortune lay at my feet. Enough to feed me and Gran for the rest of our lives!

Gran was still sound asleep, though the sky was lightening. Lately she slept until after I left for the mines, but I was so excited, I wanted to wake her and show her our fortune. This was my destiny, to be rich and fat and happy!

A shadowy movement caught the corner of my eye. I jerked around and saw a figure ducking beneath the window. I ran to the door and stepped outside. Two people were running down the street. Against the rising sun they were just two black shapes, but I knew those hulking outlines well. Frederick and Bruno.

I started to shake. All the excitement drained from me. I didn't care why they had come here or what trick they had been waiting to play. I was only worried about one thing.

Had they seen the gold?

# CHAPTER SEVEN

## Gold Means Food

I tucked the gold beneath my blankets. The warm happiness I had felt at seeing all that gold fizzled as fast as snow on a hot griddle. Now I had a weighty, guilty, heart-pounding, sick-to-my-stomach dread.

I didn't leave for the mines when I should have. I sat on top of the gold and thought of all the things that could happen. Frederick and Bruno might think I stole the gold. If they told, I could be arrested. I could go to the dungeons for the rest of my life, or even *lose* my life.

I had to tell Gran. Gran would know what to do. But when she rose from her bed, she looked so old and tired, so pale and stooped. I couldn't tell her. Any more weight on those shoulders and Gran would crumple to the ground. And I remembered the way she had reacted when I first found the spinning wheel. She did not want me to spin, and now I realized it wasn't because I couldn't do it, but because I could spin more than thread or yarn. I could spin straw into gold. And Gran had tried to keep me from doing it. What kind of magic was this?

No, I could not tell Gran. But I needed to tell someone because I felt heavy with worry, and I wouldn't know whether my worry was real or not until I said it out loud to someone. The only person I could think of to tell was Red.

When Gran wasn't looking, I removed the bobbin from the spinning wheel, wrapped it in a rag, and tied it to my waist.

I didn't see Frederick or Bruno in the mines. Any other day this would have made me happy, but today it made me anxious.

The pixies swarmed around me more than ever. When I threw dirt over my head, they'd fly away for a minute or two, but they always came back. So I just let them crawl all over me, their tiny chant ringing in my ears: "Gold, gold, gold!"

"Wow, look at him! Look at the pixies!" said a little girl working closest to me along the sluice. "You must be finding *hoards* of gold."

I didn't find a speck.

When the sun was low, I waited for Red to come out of the tunnels. She had dirt smeared all over her face and looked cross. She walked right past me but I still followed her.

"What do you want?" she asked.

"I want to show you something."

"Show me, then."

I looked around, wary. "And I need to tell you something."

She walked even faster. "So tell me something."

"It has to be someplace where no one will see or hear"— I brushed the pixies out of my eyes—"and where there are as few pixies as possible."

Red scowled at me and kept walking. But after a while she stopped and turned back. "Hurry up, I'm hungry."

I followed Red down the mountainside and through The Village. When we passed the mill, I got a cold prickle on my neck, like someone was watching me. I hurried past.

I guess I shouldn't have been surprised when Red went into The Woods, but it was getting cold and dark. I stopped just inside the trees.

"Where are we going?" I asked.

"To a place where no one will hear or see, and where there are no pixies. That *is* what you want, isn't it?" Red folded her arms impatiently.

"Is it safe?" I asked.

"If you stay on the path. And don't ask questions."

"What path?" I looked down and my mouth fell open. There was a path beneath my feet, clearly trodden and winding farther into The Woods. I would have sworn it hadn't been there before. I had never seen it. "How—?" I started, but Red cut me off.

"I said, don't ask questions." I closed my mouth and followed.

Red led us deep into The Woods, much deeper than I'd usually go. She didn't seem afraid, though. In fact, she seemed more comfortable here than she was in The Village. She touched the trees as if they were friends. A bird fluttered down to a low branch and chirped as though he were saying something to Red, and I had the feeling she understood the bird, even though she pretended not to notice.

"Do you come here often?" I asked. Red glared at me. "Sorry." I wasn't supposed to ask questions, but questions were all that rose to my mind.

The path curved and twisted. Where was she taking me and how much farther was it? I bit my tongue to keep in the questions. Then I started to hear something, a low hum. It got louder as we walked. Suddenly we rounded a corner and came upon a giant fallen tree. The tree was swarming with bees. I froze. I saw Red's thinking, of course. Bees and pixies don't like each other, so where you find a swarm of one, you probably won't find the other. But bee stings didn't sound much better than pixie bites. I stayed far back.

Red walked right to the edge of the swarm. Slowly, like a creeping cat, she moved through the buzzing wall of bees, reached her hand down the log, and pulled out a chunk of honeycomb, dripping with golden honey. She moved back just as slowly. Bees crawled all over her head and arms and even her face, but she didn't flinch, and soon they all flew away, back to their honey log. She broke the honeycomb in half and gave me a piece. "Gold you can eat," she said, and we licked the sticky mess.

"You could trade this for grain," I said. "Probably lots."

"Wouldn't want to," said Red.

"Why?" She could get a whole sack of grain for just this one chunk of honeycomb.

"Because some things people like to keep to themselves. This has always been my tree, and I don't want anyone else to know about it. If you tell, I'll punch your teeth out."

It made me feel really special that she would share it with me.

"And don't think you can come here without me, either."

"I won't."

"Promise?"

"Promise." Even if I dared to walk this far into The Woods alone, I wouldn't be able to get the honeycomb like she did, not without getting stung a thousand times.

We sucked all the honey off and chewed the waxy comb. Then we licked our fingers. It was so sweet I almost forgot why we had come here until Red pointed at the bundle tied to my waist and asked, "What did you want to show me?"

I untied the bobbin and held it out for her to see. She glanced at it, then stared blankly at me. "It was my mother's," I said.

Red raised her eyebrows, suddenly interested. "She was a spinner. From Yonder."

I looked at her, confused. "Yonder?" Gran never told me my mother was from Yonder, and she didn't tell me about the spinning until I found the wheel. It made me mad that Red knew these things and I didn't. "How do you know that? How did you know she was a spinner?"

"Some people know," she said, not looking at me, and I could tell she was hiding something.

"What people?"

"*Some* people," she said, and her nostrils flared.

"The bobbin," I said. "I think it's special." I didn't want to say "magic." I knew how Red felt about that.

"It's just a bobbin," she said.

"But special, maybe."

"How's it special? What does it do?"

I chose my words carefully. "I think it spins things different. Makes things change."

"Bobbins don't spin. They just catch whatever you're spinning." Then her eyes widened as though she suddenly realized something. "What did you spin?"

"Nothing," I said quickly. "I just . . . What if you could spin one thing into something different, not just wool into yarn?"

"Such as?"

"Such as . . . What if you could take some . . . straw and spin . . . uh . . . gold?"

Red stared at me. I couldn't tell what she was thinking.

"We need gold. Wouldn't that be great?"

"Maybe."

She didn't believe me. "If a cow can give milk and

chickens can lay eggs and dragons can make fire, then why can't a *magic* bobbin make gold?"

"Because this bobbin isn't magic," she said. "But *you* might be."

"Me? Magic? No, I'm not." Using magic was one thing. *Being* magic sounded like a mountain of disaster.

"If anything changes to gold when you spin, it's coming from inside of you, not the bobbin."

"How do you know?"

"I'm just guessing."

"Well, maybe you're guessing *wrong*."

Red sighed. "It doesn't really matter where the magic is coming from. What matters is that it's magic, and magic makes trouble. Your mother used magic to spin and she got into a lot of trouble because of it. There's always a consequence for using magic."

"But this would be a good consequence," I said. "Gold."

"Yes, but—"

"And gold would solve a lot of problems." Stomach problems, for sure.

"Maybe, *but*—"

"And it's not like I want it all for myself—"

Red hit me on the head so I would stop talking. "Those are just the natural, regular consequences, Rump. There will be magical consequences too. Magic has its own rules."

"How do you know? Don't tell me it's just a guess."

Red gritted her teeth. "Didn't you learn anything when you watched Kessler get chased by every mouse on The Mountain?"

"But nothing happened when I spun! I didn't catch on fire or get attacked by mice! I just made gold! Fat skeins of gold that could feed the whole village!" I clapped my hands over my mouth, but Red didn't look surprised.

"Rump," she said in a soft voice, "does anyone else know about this?"

I sighed. "Frederick and Bruno were looking through my window this morning, right after I spun the gold."

Red frowned.

"But," I went on, if only to make myself feel better, "they probably didn't know what they were seeing. Probably just looked like a pile of yarn to them."

Red's frown deepened.

And that's when I realized what kind of worry I had. The worry went from my head and sunk down to my chest and settled to a sickness in my stomach. Frederick and Bruno might be complete idiots, but any village idiot knows gold when they see it.

The next rations day, the line at the mill was very long. Everyone was eager to stock up before winter came, and it was almost here. The air was biting now. There was always frost in the mornings. The pixies were more subdued, and they began building nests for their winter sleep. Now we were just waiting for the snow.

When it was my turn, the miller gave me a sack of meal, bigger than usual. I looked at him, surprised. No one else got this much meal.

"Gold means food," the miller said gleefully.

I looked at him, confused. I had found only a few pebbles of gold in the last week. And the miller wasn't kind or generous.

I opened the sack just outside the cottage and a thick, dusty powder billowed out. I choked and coughed as the dust went into my lungs. The miller had filled the bag with chalk and sawdust.

*Gold means food.*

The miller was giving me a message.

# CHAPTER EIGHT

## Gold Means Secrets

I did not know what to do. We needed food. The miller had the food and he wanted gold. I had lots of gold, spun into perfect little coils with my mother's spinning wheel. Spun with magic that Red insisted was dangerous.

"Where are the rations?" Gran asked. I was empty-handed, having thrown away the sack full of sawdust.

"I suppose I didn't find enough gold," I said, looking at my feet.

"Well, I'll go give that miller a piece of my mind." Gran rose up from her chair, then staggered and fell back.

"Gran!" I rushed to her, but she waved me away.

"Only a little dizzy spell." She closed her eyes and took a few breaths. Her hands shook. She needed food. I would have to take some of the gold to the miller. Maybe I could mix the coils with some dirt and other gold flecks and pebbles from the mines. He might not notice the difference. But a dark feeling rose in me. If the miller was as greedy as he seemed, he would notice. So I kept the gold hidden and hoped that the miller had only made a mistake with the sack of sawdust.

"We will make do," Gran said. "We have the chickens and the goat. So we won't starve."

We killed one of our two hens. The meat would have to last us until the next rations day.

Gran and I ate in silence. Eating the chicken should have been a celebration, a great luxury, but we were both melancholy. My gaze kept wandering over to the spinning wheel and to my bed, where the gold was hidden.

Gran followed my gaze. "I hope you haven't touched that wheel," she said. "You don't know how to work it properly. You could hurt yourself."

"Did my mother hurt herself?" I asked. The question flew out of me without warning.

Gran froze with a bit of chicken raised to her mouth. She lowered her hands. "Why would you ask such a thing?"

"Why didn't you tell me she was from Yonder?"

"Who told you that?" Gran asked.

"Red."

"Red. Yes, well, her grandmother . . ."

"What did my mother spin?" I asked.

Gran stiffened. "What did she spin? What do people usually spin? Why—? Have you—?" She looked from the wheel back to me. I could see her struggling, trying to decide what to say.

"Your mother spun trouble," she said, "and then left it on my hands."

"Is that how you think of me?" I asked. "As the trouble she left?"

"Oh, child."

"Rump!" I shouted. "My name is Rump!"

Gran's eyes were shiny with tears. "You are my grandson, Rump. I have always loved you. I have always tried to protect you, and I will do my best to protect you now. Do not concern yourself with your mother or her spinning wheel. It will only bring you sorrow."

I didn't ask any more. I felt strange, like things had shifted around me when I wasn't looking, but I didn't know what it meant.

The strangeness crept into my dream that night. A woman was spinning by the fireplace. She had long black hair and green eyes, like mine. I had never seen this woman before, but I knew she was my mother. She was spinning straw into gold.

She smiled at the gold at first, and the glittering skeins piled around her feet, like a golden pool. But as the pile grew larger, her smile faded. Her spinning slowed and seemed to be difficult, but still she spun. The pile grew and grew and grew, spreading wider and rising higher.

When the gold reached my mother's chin, she looked panicked, like she was submerged in water and didn't know how to swim. When it reached her eyes, they were full of fear. Finally, the gold covered her whole head, and I couldn't see her anymore. But the pile of gold still grew.

When it reached the ceiling, I woke up.

# CHAPTER NINE

## Gold Found, Treasure Lost

Rations day came again at last. I went outside, eager to get an early start, and was showered with sparkling white. Winter had arrived. At first I was happy, because a fresh blanket of snow made the world look peaceful and new. Nothing bad could happen in such fluffy white. But then the cold bit my skin and I remembered what winter really meant.

It meant that soon the pass up The Mountain would be closed. No one would be able to get through to trade gold for food. It meant slow, grueling work in a frozen mine. It meant cold and hunger—more hunger than usual.

Milk gave only drippings of milk, our one remaining hen had no eggs, and Nothing bellowed at me because his hooves were frozen to the ground. When I finally pawed him loose with icy fingers, he kicked me from behind and I landed face-first in the snow.

I hate winter.

When I arrived at the mines, Frederick threw a snowball at my face. Bruno got me on the back of the head. Then a tree branch dumped a load of snow down the neck of my shirt.

Winter hates me.

It was a long day in the mines. I kept myself from going crazy by making up rhymes.

*Frozen fingers,*
*Frozen toes*
*Where are you, gold?*
*Nobody knows.*
*Spin a sock, spin a hat*
*Spin a stupid, ugly rat*
*A furry cat*
*A winged bat*
*Spin them in a tasty stew*
*I like the sound of that!*

I went to the mill for my rations and waited in the long line with a grumbling stomach. I had found a little more gold than usual this week. I think it helped that the pixies were now sleeping for the winter. If gold meant food, then the miller would have to give me my rations. But when I reached the front of the line, he simply looked down at me over his bulging belly and said, "No gold, no food." His eyes had a greedy gleam. He *knew.*

I understood my dream now. I hadn't spun that much gold, but it was already choking me.

When I came home, Gran was still in bed. Her eyes were open, but she just stared up at the ceiling.

"Gran?"

She blinked but didn't look at me or speak.

"Gran? Are you all right?" I walked to her and placed my hand on her cheek. I pulled away quickly. Her skin was so hot it burned my cold palm.

I stumbled backward and fell, then ran outside and down the road to Red's house. I didn't know anywhere else to go. I pounded on the door, hoping someone was home.

A woman swung open the door, brandishing a wooden spoon. Red's mother. She looked fierce, just like Red, but she gave a start when she saw me panting and crying.

"Rump?" Red peered out from behind her mother.

"My gran . . . something's wrong. Please . . ."

Red's mother threw down her spoon and grabbed her cloak. "Come," she said. Red followed, and we ran back to the cottage.

When we walked in, Red's mother went right to Gran. "Elsbith . . ." She gently touched Gran's forehead. "Red, go outside and get a bucket of snow."

I stood by the bed while Red's mother looked Gran over. Gran opened her eyes and made a little gurgling sound, but she didn't speak. It was like she was trying to say something, but the words were heavy and got twisted on her tongue.

"What's wrong with her?" I asked.

Red's mother didn't look at me. "She's old."

"But what's wrong with her?"

"Oh, child." She looked at me now, and her eyes were so full of pity I thought I might be sick. "No one can keep going forever. She's ill. Her brain isn't working right."

Her brain! I needed Gran's brain!

"Can you help her? Will she get better?"

She gave me a tragic smile. "We'll just have to see."

My whole body sagged, and she touched my shoulder. "It will be all right."

Red and her mother placed cold cloths on Gran's face and rubbed warm ones on her feet. They boiled water and the leftover chicken bones and spooned the broth in Gran's mouth. A lot just dripped down her cheeks and chin, but Gran seemed a little more awake while we fed her. She looked at me, or at least I thought she did, and then she fell asleep.

"She should sleep for the night," said Red's mother. She picked up her cloak and went to the door. "I'll be back in the morning. Come, Red."

"I'll be there in a moment." Red's mother nodded and shut the door.

Red only waited a few seconds before she did what I knew she would: boss me.

"I know what you're thinking, but you can't."

"How do you know what I'm thinking? I'm an idiot, remember? I don't think that much."

Red's eyes saddened. "I don't think you're an idiot, Rump."

"Well, you'd be the only one." Including myself. I *was*

an idiot. Why did I have to spin all that straw into gold? I should have listened to Gran. But maybe trading the gold for food could make her better.

"Rump, don't trade the gold."

"What makes you think I would?" I glared at Red and she backed away a little. *Red*, backing away from *me*.

"Things will turn out all right," she said. "But not if you trade that gold. It's not safe."

I sat by the fire, picked up bits of straw, and flung them into the flames. "Just go away."

"Rump—"

"Just leave me alone!" I shouted.

Red breathed in sharply and opened the door. A cold gust blew in and made me shiver. "I take it back. You *are* an idiot!" And she slammed the door.

I sat in front of the fire until it was cold ash.

I didn't sleep all night. And when the village bell chimed for the mining day to begin, I didn't go. I stayed by Gran's side and fed her broth. She still didn't speak or look at me, but I got the broth in her mouth and she swallowed.

She needed more food. She couldn't get well without more food.

When Gran fell asleep after dark, I went to my bed and took out three skeins of gold. I wrapped them in a dirty rag and tucked them inside my jacket. Then I walked outside and headed toward the mill.

Gold meant food.

Opal was the one who answered the door. She stared at me with her blank face.

"I want to see the miller," I said.

Her tongue stretched and wound around her mouth. "What for?" she asked. It was the first time I'd ever heard Opal speak. She sounded annoyed.

"I have something for him. Something he'll want to trade me."

"Rations day was yesterday. Father doesn't trade unless it's rations day."

"He'll want to trade me now," I said.

Her tongue flicked out. "Come back next rations day." She started to close the door, but a deep voice sounded behind her.

"Opal, who are you talking to?" Opal shrank back in the doorway, and Oswald the miller filled it up with his huge girth. He was almost as wide as he was tall. His belt strained on the last notch.

"Oh, it's you, then, is it? We've no rations for you, and we're all tightening our belts. Begone."

I tried to speak, but my tongue felt heavy inside my mouth, like it had swelled and hardened. I figured what I carried would speak louder than words, anyway, so I took the bundle from my jacket and revealed the gold.

Quickly the miller stepped close, blocking the gold from Opal's view. He looked from side to side, making sure no one else was around, then lowered his big nose to my bundle. His fat face spread wide, and the gold glinted in his greedy eyes.

He reached for one of the skeins, but I pulled away. I thought of all the things I could demand, all the food. I would ask him to take me into the storehouse and let me choose as much as I wanted: honey, oats, apples, onions, carrots. He would mill my grain to a fine powder. But my tongue was so heavy and the words would not come.

"What will you give me?" I said in a strangled voice. "What will you give me for this?"

The miller smiled as if he felt my struggle. "Clever boy," he said. "Opal, go and get a sack of flour and a sack of oats. Ten pounds each."

I wanted to say that wasn't fair. I had three skeins of gold. That should be worth more than twenty pounds of food. I should get salt, honey, at least a little meat, but I couldn't say it. It was as if the gold were pressing down on my tongue.

When Opal came back with the food, she placed it at my feet. She looked from her father to me. She stared at the bundle in my arms, now covered up. "Leave us, Opal," said Oswald. She licked her lips and then hurried away.

I held out the gold like a dumb puppet, and the miller snatched it from my hands. "Such a clever boy," said the miller, adding sugar to his oily voice, but instead of sweet he sounded rancid.

I heaved the food onto my back and took it home. I made a runny mush with the oats and held a spoonful to Gran's mouth. She twitched when the food touched her mouth and turned away.

"It's food, Gran. You have to eat."

"Where . . . ?" Her question trailed away.

"Shhh. Just eat." I spooned the food into her mouth, willing her to get better.

Gran's fever raged for the next three days. I made more of the oat mush, biscuits, and bread soaked in milk, but she wouldn't eat. She was so thin I thought she might sink right into the mattress. Soon she would just be straw.

I kept talking to Gran aloud, pressing a cool cloth to her forehead and hoping that she would respond. One day faded into another as I told her stories, all the stories she had told me about witches, and trolls, and wolves, and ogres. I talked late into the night, until I had repeated every story I knew a dozen times, so tonight I told a real story. The story about me. I told it just the way she had told me, how I was born and my name and my unknown destiny.

"And now I have a spinning wheel," I said as I reached the end. "From my mother. And I can spin gold. I can spin straw into gold, just like my mother. Did she show you her gold? Did she tell you about her magic? She gave it to me." It suddenly struck me how different things would be if my mother had lived. All that was wrong could be set right. I'd know my whole name and I'd understand my destiny.

Gran's eyes flew open, and she grabbed my arm with

a surprisingly firm grip. She gurgled a little, trying to speak.

My heart leapt. Gran was getting well! "Gran?" I asked. "What is it?"

She gurgled some more, and then, with great effort, she said my name. "Wah . . . Wah . . . Wump . . . my boy . . ."

"Yes, Gran, I'm here." I held her frail, gnarled hands tight in mine.

Gran's eyes didn't move, but they filled with tears, which rolled down the sides of her wrinkled cheeks. "You . . . spin." Slowly she raised a trembling hand and placed it on my chest, right over my heart. "Spin . . . gold . . . here." She tapped on my chest. "Gold . . . here." She closed her eyes then, but gently muttered, "Spin, spin, spin."

I tried to spoon more food into her mouth, but she wouldn't take it. She kept muttering, "Spin, spin, spin."

Soon Gran was asleep again.

In the morning, she did not wake.

# CHAPTER TEN

## Unfair Bargains

The bell chimed and the gnomes ran through the village shouting, "Elsbith, grandmother of Rump, has gone the way of all the earth!"

The gnomes announced death as they did anything else, with squeaking excitement, and that morning I despised the pudgy, waddling creatures more than ever. I went outside and threw snowballs at every gnome that passed. I missed them all.

If there was ever a time to cry, this was it, but I couldn't. Everything inside me felt shriveled up and hollow, like a dead tree. I didn't cry when I saw that Gran would not wake. I didn't cry when they came and covered her with her quilt and took her away. I didn't cry when she was lowered into the hard, frozen earth. I didn't cry when Red's mother touched my shoulder and placed in my arms a loaf of still-warm bread.

When I came home, the cottage looked like a chicken coop attacked by a fox. Feathers and bones everywhere. Oats and flour sprinkled across the floor. Straw and dirt, pots and dishes and rags. Buckets of melted snow leaked on the ground, creating little muddy rivers. It looked like I felt. Torn to shreds.

Gran's bed was empty, the indents of her small body still pressed in the mattress.

That's when I cried. I cried real snot-running, chest-heaving cries until it was all drained out and I was empty, empty, empty. Gran was gone. She would never greet me with a rhyme, or comfort me when I felt small. She would never sit by the fire and tell me stories.

I sat in the middle of the mess. I was still holding the loaf of bread Red's mother had given me. Mindlessly, I tore chunks off and ate, swallowing huge pieces before I chewed. I ate and ate. I ate the entire loaf, and still I was empty, empty, empty.

The spinning wheel sat motionless by the snuffed-out fire. The wheel felt like a giant eye looming over me. I went to my bed and ripped open my mattress, letting the gold spill out onto the floor. It glimmered with cruel coldness.

I hated that gold. I wanted nothing to do with it. I gathered every last skein inside my blanket and hauled it to the mill. This time the miller was waiting for me.

"Such a sad time for you," he said with false sympathy, "but it seems that good fortune has befallen you in other ways." His eyes narrowed on my heavy bundle. I flung it down at his feet and let the gold spill all over his doorstep.

The miller jumped back and then smiled. "My, my, you have been busy."

"What will you give me?" I asked.

"Here." He handed me a small sack of potatoes, maybe five pounds. "Food is always more expensive in the winter, but keep up the hard work. I will always give you a fair bargain."

I stared at the miller, seething. I wanted to say he was a lying, cheating, despicable, heartless villain. I wanted to throw the potatoes in his fat face and take my gold back. But my jaw was clamped shut, and my arms were fastened tight around the bag.

The miller bent down and scooped up the gold. Then he shut the door in my speechless face.

This wasn't magic. It was a curse, and I could feel it wrapping around me fast now, tightening its coils.

I thought I wouldn't spin again, but eventually my food ran out. I had killed the last hen, and Milk was not giving enough milk to quench thirst, let alone live on. It was pointless to look for gold in the mines. Even if I found some, I knew the miller would still give me nothing. He wanted *my* gold.

So as time wore on, I was forced to spin more. I gathered bits of straw from the floor and the hens' nest outside, but all that got me was some shriveled turnips and onions. When the last turnip was gone, I tore open Gran's mattress and started spinning the straw inside.

I spun Gran's entire straw mattress into gold. At first, I cried as I did it. I was betraying Gran and spinning her memory away all at once. But then I stopped crying. I stopped worrying that anything bad would happen, and I stopped hoping that anything good would happen. I think I stopped feeling anything at all. I just spun.

For four months, I spun and traded the gold to the miller. The trade was never fair, but I never argued. Once, I traded ten skeins of gold for a small sack of flour and some rotten carrots. Soon I found I didn't care how fair the bargains were. Trading the gold became more of a habit than a need.

I no longer went to the mines. I never even went outside unless I was going to the mill, but no one seemed to notice or care, except Red. She visited me sometimes, though we said very little. Once in a while, she brought a loaf of bread from her mother. That's the only time I felt anything. It's hard not to feel guilty when starving people bring you food.

I thought I would just live that way for the rest of my life, spinning gold and never getting rich, eating food and never getting full. Or tall, or smart, or kind, or anything at all.

Maybe it would have stayed that way forever if a certain visitor had not come to The Mountain in search of a certain kind of gold.

# CHAPTER ELEVEN

## King Barf

As winter melted away, the creatures of The Mountain began to emerge from their long slumber. I woke one morning to a pixie on my nose. It seemed the pixies had nested in my chimney, and now that they were waking, the whole cottage had become one big, swarming pixie nest. I tried to swat them away from the tangles of gold all over the floor, but they shrieked and bit me. I ran outside. The air was still chilly, but at least I could breathe without my tongue freezing.

Then I noticed something strange. The villagers should have all been at work in the mines by now, but instead, everyone was gathering in the village square. The crowds were just visible from my cottage, down the street and in front of the mill. It seemed the whole village was there, chattering and buzzing, as excited as the pixies inside.

I found Red, walking with her mother toward the square.

"What's going on?" I asked.

"Mountain pass is open," she said.

"So?"

She pointed down The Mountain. "Someone's coming up."

A big open sound rang through the air, like the village bell, but deeper and longer. It sounded again and again with a regular rhythm.

"It's a royal procession," said a woman.

"A what? What for?"

The most royal visitor we ever received was the tax collector, and he never brought a procession.

I looked down the road winding up The Mountain and saw the most amazing sight. A dozen horses, two dozen! And not little horses from The Mountain, but big warhorses from The Kingdom. And on those horses were soldiers dressed in red-and-gold tunics, with spears and swords and bows and arrows.

We waited. Everyone was whispering excitedly, guessing at who it could be and why they were coming.

"Maybe there's a war," said Frederick, "and they need soldiers."

"Maybe we haven't been sending enough gold for the king's liking," said a woman, which I thought probably closer to the truth.

The procession finally reached The Village. A soldier lifted a golden horn to his mouth and blew three high notes. Pixies fluttered all around the horn.

"Announcing His Royal Majesty, King Bartholomew Archibald Reginald Fife!"

The villagers all gasped in unison. Everyone whispered to each other. Never before had a king come to visit The Mountain. Everyone hushed as the soldiers parted and the king came forward.

My entire life, whenever I heard mention of his name—King Bartholomew Archibald Reginald Fife—I imagined someone very big and very handsome and very brainy. I think everyone did. But now that I saw him, "King Barf" almost seemed more fitting.

If I had just looked at his royal costume, I suppose I could have been impressed, though gold wasn't so impressive to me anymore. King Barf wore a gold crown on his head, gold chains around his neck, gold armor on his chest, gold rings on all his fingers. His saddle was gilded gold. His boots had gold buckles. I imagined if I could see beneath his horse's hooves, the horseshoes would be gold. Gold, gold, gleaming gold. There were servants on all sides of the king with giant paddles, and they swatted at the pixies trying to converge on the king and all his glorious gold.

But King Bartholomew Archibald Reginald Fife . . .

King Barf was chubby.

He had a turned-up nose and floppy ears.

He looked like a pink pig with a crown on his head.

"My people of The Mountain," he said, double chins wobbling. He sounded like a pig with a stuffy nose. "Your work is so valuable to The Kingdom.

"I have traveled here personally to your village because a curiosity has come to my attention." King Barf pulled something from his saddlebag, and the blood drained from my face. He held up a single spool of thread. Gold threads perfectly coiled. My gold!

"For several years now, I have received little gold for your tax. I am a generous king and I have sustained you, yet lo and behold, I find this gold, brought to me by one of my own advisers. Fine gold. Fine workmanship. And yet no one in The Kingdom seems to know where it came from."

My gold. The miller. When I traded it, I didn't think about what he would *do* with it, where it would end up. But how could I *not* have seen this? Of course, he would trade the gold in The Kingdom. And the king, loving gold as he did, would get his hands on it eventually, and then, of course, he would wonder. It wasn't normal gold dug out of The Mountain in clumps and pebbles, mixed with dirt. No craftsman could have molded the gold into such fine threads. This was gold only I could spin.

King Barf's piggy eyes turned cold and suspicious. "My soldiers will search through your homes and your mines to be sure that you are not robbing me of my rights to the gold in my kingdom. If I find you are deceiving me, stealing from me . . ." He squeezed the gold tight in his hand. He didn't crush it or make it disappear, but we understood.

A murmur went through the crowd until the soldier blew his horn again. "All citizens of The Mountain will go to their homes and await inspection!" Everyone hustled and bustled against one another, all moving in different directions.

I stood still. I could feel Red staring at me. Finally, I looked at her, and for the first time since we had worked side by side in the sluices, Red hit me. She slapped me right over the head and said, "You really are a numbskull," and she trudged off.

Was there any point in arguing?

I was doomed. There was gold lying in tangles on my floor as if it were nothing but straw. I hadn't even bothered to hide it. And what about the miller? Did he still have gold sitting in his house? Surely he had hidden it well, or he was making some kind of plan. I could hide mine too, in The Woods. Maybe near Red's hollow beehive log. I didn't care about the gold, but I didn't want to go to the dungeons for the rest of my life or sit in the stocks so people could throw mud and rotten food at me.

I raced home. I gathered all the skeins and tangles and bits of gold that I could find, wrapped them in a rag, and ran out the back door. A few pixies that were outside flitted over and started sniffing and chattering around the bundle. *Don't swat them. Don't cause commotion. If I let them be, then no one will notice.*

I crept through trees and huddled behind rocks, away from roads and paths where soldiers were going in and out of houses. The gnomes were running around madly with messages from soldiers to the king, only gnomes have a hard time with longer names and messages, so King Barf's name always came out a little garbled.

"Message for King Barf-a-hew Archy-baldy Regy-naldy Fife!"

"No gold here!"

"No gold there!"

"No gold!"

"No gold!"

"No gold!"

I walked slowly. I was so small, no one would notice me—as long as I didn't panic. I passed the village square and approached the mill, where the miller stood outside with his nine sons and Opal. Three soldiers were about to go inside, but the miller didn't look nervous. Maybe he'd already traded all the gold. But when he caught sight of me creeping toward the trees with my suspicious little bundle, his eyes went wide with horror. I shook my head and tried to point in the direction of The Woods. I could slip by. If he kept the soldiers' attention, they wouldn't notice me.

But the pixies noticed me. All the gold in my bundle was just too much to hide from them. They flew to me one by one, and the sound grew. It started as a soft twitter, like the distant chirping of birds, and then built to a high, steady hum.

Then there was silence.

It was the kind of silence that lasts only a moment or two, but feels like a hundred hours because you're just waiting for something awful to happen.

I remember when I had this idea that I could fly. I built myself wings out of sticks and chicken feathers, and I climbed a high rock and jumped. I didn't fly. I broke my arm. But that wasn't the worst part. The worst part was just the moment before, when I went from the exhilaration of soaring through the air to the horror of plummeting toward the hard earth. I knew I was going to hit the ground and feel pain.

This was like that moment. The moment before everything went bad.

When the pixies attacked, I flung my arms up and swatted at them. I swung my bundle of gold. I clawed at the ground, flinging mud and dirt and snow in all directions. Finally, the pixies were gone and everything was quiet again. Even quieter than before.

I took stock of myself. I still had my bundle of gold tight in my hand. I turned around. The miller and his nine ugly sons and his one pretty daughter and the three soldiers all stared at me, and then at something on the ground. I followed their eyes, and my stomach twisted. There on the ground was a spool of gold, unraveling toward the soldiers.

The spool rolled again and again and my life unraveled before my eyes, one roll for every year. I snatched up the gold, clutching it to my chest, then I turned and ran for The Woods. I don't know why I thought I could run, but I was going to, until a giant horse blocked my path and there were shiny black boots right in my face. Boots with giant gold buckles.

King Barf looked down at me, and his piggy eyes narrowed on the gold I still clutched in my hands. He sniffed, as if he could smell the rest of the gold in my bundle.

"Well, well," he said. "The pixies seem to find you even more enchanting than they do me. How fascinating."

# CHAPTER TWELVE

## The Miller's Lie

"Give me the gold in your hands," said King Barf.

The miller stepped in front of me and gave me a warning look. "The gold is mine, Your Majesty," he blurted.

"Yours?" said the king and I in unison, but nobody seemed to notice me just then.

"I asked the boy to bring it. He's my servant. Come here, boy, quick. Bring the rest!" he snapped.

I didn't move. What trick was he playing? He would certainly be punished for hiding gold. Why would he risk his neck for me?

"Move, boy! Excuse him, Your Majesty. He's a half-wit. Doesn't know his own name!" The miller laughed and his big belly jiggled.

"No," said the king. "Give the gold to me. All of it."

I tried to move but my legs grew roots into the ground.

My tongue swelled and my brain fuzzed. I don't know why I said it, but the words just spilled out.

"What will you give me?" I covered my mouth, and everyone gasped. The air grew still and cold. King Barf moved his horse so close to me that the tip of his sword was level with my nose.

"Give me the gold and I will spare your life," said the king, his nasal voice now quiet and dangerous.

Slowly, trembling, I held out the gold to King Barf and he snatched it from me. He examined the skein, and then he opened the bundle and stared inside for a long time. Finally, he pulled out another spool of thread. He stretched the gold in his beefy hands and moved it back and forth, watching it gleam in the sunlight.

"How is this done?" King Barf asked, holding out the gold to the miller. I had become invisible again.

"Well, see . . . Your Majesty . . . 'tis a strange business. Full of mystery and, and . . . and magic."

The king stiffened. Not many people tolerated magic, and King Barf not at all. He didn't like anything that might have more power than he did.

"Not the witchy kind," said the miller quickly. "A good kind . . . magic that makes good things. You see, my daughter here—she's not just a beauty, she's talented too—spins with a touch of magic. She can spin straw into gold!"

My mouth dropped and so did Opal's. Her blank face became horrified. She looked from her father to the king, back and forth, her tongue whipping out again and again.

King Barf didn't even glance at Opal. He simply held

the gold up to the sun, turned it so it caught the light, and smiled. "I have heard of those who can spin more than just wool or cotton. I have never seen it. Show me."

"Oh, but you see her work in your hands!" said the miller.

"Show me the spinning. Show me how she turns it into gold."

"Oh. Well." The miller laughed nervously, as if he hadn't expected this. "That's part of the magic, Your Majesty. Not even I have seen her do it, and she does it right in my own house. But, mark me, you give her a pile of straw, a roomful of straw, and the next morning she's spun it to gold! 'Tis a marvel." The miller gave me the tiniest glance, and then, "We can spin you more, this very evening."

King Barf finally looked at Opal and appraised her. Opal stood frozen and pale, not even her tongue flicked out. She was so pretty, I might have believed she really could spin straw to gold, but I knew that she couldn't. And so did she. Opal began to tremble.

"Why have I not heard of your daughter's marvelous gift before?" asked King Barf. "Such talents would bring me great pleasure and would be rewarded openly if I did not think it was deceitful. If I did not think you were trying to steal from me."

The miller blathered. "Oh no, Your Majesty . . . Yes, Your Majesty . . . Of course, no . . . Yes, not to worry. We mean no deception. We are humble, honest subjects. We live only to serve. My daughter has just discovered this gift. It is something that has grown with her, grown with her beauty. We merely brought the gold for trading to make sure it would hold its value, to know that it was real so that we might present a tribute to you and know that the gold was worthy of you, Your Majesty. Never to deceive you, Your Majesty."

The king waved one of his soldiers to come forth and issued a command in his ear. The soldier went and stood beside Opal.

"It pleases me that your daughter should accompany me to my castle," said the king. Opal looked up, her wide eyes full of terror.

The miller gaped. "Well, I . . . I . . . well, yes . . . 'twould be an honor, Your Majesty, but see—"

"If what you say is true," said King Barf, "you and your family and all The Mountain shall be rewarded. But if not, the punishment for deceiving the king is severe. Dungeons or death."

Opal was pulled up onto a horse and led away with the king's procession. King Barf cradled the bundle of gold like a baby to his chest. He looked back at the miller with a triumphant grin. I couldn't see Opal's face before she disappeared.

The miller swayed and his sons gathered around him. "Oh, what have I done? What have I done? What have I done?" He buried his face in his hands.

I never liked the miller Oswald. He was a liar and a cheat and greedy. It was his fault that his daughter was being led to her doom. But, no, that wasn't true. It was *my* fault. *I* was the greedy one. I had spun the gold. I had traded the gold. I had fumbled and tripped and spilled the gold. Now Opal was all spun into the mess and she hadn't done anything at all. Poor, beautiful Opal. That thought poured icy water over my head. An innocent girl was being led to her doom because of me.

A pixie fluttered up to me, shaking her fists and squealing as if she were reprimanding me. The pixie bit my nose, and in a minute it swelled so large I had to breathe through my mouth. Now my nose was bigger than my face.

I guess I deserved that.

It was still morning, but no one was working in the mines now. Everyone was scattered around the town, buzzing about King Barf and all his soldiers. A gnome ran past my feet and down the road chanting, "The king is gone! The king is gone! He took the miller's daughter along!"

Gran once said there would be times in my life when I would be trapped, with walls all around me too high to climb and no way out. Then I would need someone from outside and above to throw down a rope and pull me up. I believed Gran; I just always thought that she would be the one to throw the rope.

I needed help. I needed advice. But I couldn't think of a single person in all The Mountain who could help me. Red was mad at me. The miller probably wanted to strangle me. Milk and Nothing had nothing to offer. And the magic and the gold had spun me into a bigger heap of trouble than I could have imagined.

And that's when I realized who could possibly help—the one person who might be able to give me some answers about my mother and the spinning and the magic.

I needed The Witch of The Woods.

# CHAPTER THIRTEEN

## The Witch of The Woods

I grabbed a gnome by his leg just outside The Woods. I held him upside down with both my arms. He grunted and swatted his stubby hands at me, but once I said I had a message for him to deliver, he clapped his hands and smiled, showing tiny yellow teeth. I set him down and recited my message.

For Red:
 I know you are mad at me, and this might make you madder, but I am going to see the witch.
 If I don't return, please take care of Milk and Nothing.

Rump

"Now repeat, and be quiet. Only Red should hear this."

The gnome repeated the message in a croaky little voice and then sped off to deliver it, chanting, "Message for Red! Message for Red!" over and over.

I stood on the edge of The Woods. They were so dark you could hardly tell that it was daytime, and spring's warmth seemed far away. There was a clean blanket of snow on the ground, and it was unnaturally quiet. It should have looked peaceful, but it felt eerie. My heart was pounding so hard I could feel it in my throat and ears.

I looked for the path that Red had shown me before, when we went to the honey. Something about that path made me feel a little safer, but I didn't see any sign of it. Perhaps it was hidden beneath the snow. Perhaps the witch didn't want to be found.

I started to think this was a very stupid idea.

Just as I was about to turn back, a twig snapped and Red appeared, her cheeks and nose rosy with cold and her breath raspy from running.

"What do you mean you're going to see the witch?" Red asked.

"I have to," I said.

"Rump, witches don't help with things like this. It's not that they can't. They don't like to, and even if they do, sometimes they cause *more* trouble."

"Opal is in trouble because of me." My chin began to tremble.

"Opal got taken away because her father is a greedy pig!"

"No," I said. "Because I spun all that gold. And then I traded it with the miller, even though you told me not to. And then I tried to hide the gold, but I dropped it right in front of the king!" I held my breath to keep the tears from spilling over.

Red was stunned into silence. She probably thought I was a bigger numbskull than ever. I thought she might hit me over the head again or punch me in the nose. Instead, she grabbed me by the arm and pulled me into The Woods.

"What are you doing?" I asked.

"I'm taking you to The Witch of The Woods."

"You are? You know where she lives? How?"

"Just stay on the path."

"But there isn't any . . ." I trailed off as I looked down to see the path beneath my feet again, stretching out into The Woods. Now I was certain this was a path that only revealed itself for Red.

We followed the path for a ways until dark trees surrounded us and the village had disappeared behind. This path didn't wind or wander much. It was narrow, but clear, with stones along either side.

Red walked fast and determined, still pulling me by the arm. A squirrel chirped and screeched right above my head. "Squirrel!" I squeaked, crouching down and covering my head with my arms.

Fitzgerald, a boy younger but much bigger than me, was once challenged to run into The Woods and he got attacked by mad squirrels. He still has little teeth marks all over his face and neck.

"They won't attack you," said Red. I slowly looked up and saw that the squirrel was gone. "And they never attacked Fitzgerald, either. That's the story he tells, but his scars are really just from the pox and scratching so much."

We were walking uphill now. And the farther up The Mountain we went, the colder it got. Soon snow began to fall, even though it had been warm in The Village. Big, fat flakes came and settled, threatening to cover the path if we didn't hurry. My feet were numb.

Then finally, as if it had just materialized before me, we saw a cottage, nestled in the trees, smoke rising from the chimney.

I stood frozen for a minute and I almost ran back just as fast as I had come, but the door unlatched and someone came out, hobbling bent over a stick.

I stared. My mouth hung open.

"Red, child, is that you?" said the old woman.

"Hello, Granny," said Red. "Rump wanted to see you."

My mouth ran dry. Red's granny! The Witch of The Woods! Red's granny was The Witch of The Woods!

My tongue got all wrapped around my teeth. "Y-y-you-your granny! Your granny's the W-w-w . . ."

"She's not actually a witch," Red said defensively. "She's *perceptive*."

The witch laughed. "Yes, very," she said with a wink.

"You have very good senses, Granny. Ears and eyes and nose and all. It's part of your destiny."

"Oh, and what a treat to feast my senses upon. Well, come in, my boy. I've been waiting for you. I am sorry about your gran." Red's granny didn't look how I always imagined a witch would look. She was old, of course, but she didn't have warts or green teeth and her smile was sincere and inviting. Maybe witches were supposed to be inviting, so they could lure you in to chop you to bits and put you in a stew.

"Come on. I've got stew brewing in the fire."

I stepped back again. "Stew . . . ? What kind of stew?"

"She's not going to eat you, Rump." Red shoved me forward. Then I smelled the stew. My mouth watered, it smelled so delicious. I walked in the door.

At first I saw what I would expect to see in a witch's lair. There were bottles everywhere, tiny vials to giant jugs. It was too dim to see inside of them, but I imagined they contained eyeballs, blood, snakes, or roaches. Little fingers, maybe. A hen clucked and rattled its cage in a corner. Herbs and plants and flowers hung from the ceiling. They looked very fresh, and I wondered how she managed to grow things in the frozen ground—not to mention in a haunted wood. By the fireplace there was a giant pot. That's where the witch would put all my little chopped pieces, no doubt.

The witch, or Red's granny (I didn't know how to think of her now), beckoned me over to the fire. The pot was full of broth and vegetables I hadn't seen in ages, even though I had been eating a lot. Basil, celery, onions, meat, and other smells reached my nose and made my stomach rumble.

"So," said the witch, blocking the path to the stew, "the trouble has begun."

"Begun?" I asked.

"Oh, you're just getting started, my boy." She laughed, a wheezing cackle. "Spinning gold? Bargaining with the miller? Great mountains, boy, where did you ever get such an idea? What would your mother say? Oh, how things come full circle!" She laughed some more.

"It's not funny," I said.

"No, it's not," said the witch. "It's dreadful. So dreadful I have to laugh to not cry."

I was starting to feel surly. I hadn't come here to be teased. "What do you know about my mother?"

"Sit." The witch pointed to a chair by a spinning wheel, and I froze.

"I don't want to," I said. I would never touch a spinning wheel again. Never!

The witch ladled a bowl of steaming stew and held it before my face. "I'm not asking you to spin."

"I don't want to," I said.

"Then don't. Now sit."

I sat on the floor, and she chuckled and handed me the stew. I sniffed it. Could you smell poison? Poison or not, it smelled delicious. I took a steaming spoonful and let it sit in my mouth until I had sucked out all the flavor before swallowing. I had never tasted such a wonderful stew, full of flavors I couldn't name.

"Now, then," said the witch. "Did your gran ever tell you why your mother left Yonder?"

I shook my head. "I never even knew she was from Yonder, not until Red told me."

"Hmmm. Where to begin . . . Well, I suppose the best place to start is the beginning. Your mother was a born spinner. Here, on The Mountain, we search for gold. In The Valley they farm, and in Yonder they raise sheep and gather wool. They dye their wools and they weave and knit and spin. Your mother was one of the best, an unusual spinner. She had . . . special gifts."

"You mean she was a witch," I said.

"Well, I don't think that word means what people think it means. Magic is nothing but transformation of what is already there. The gold in this very mountain is embedded in dirt and rock. How did it become gold? The earth is full of mystery and magic, and so was your mother. So, yes, in that sense she was a witch. Spinning with magic was in her blood."

I looked down at my hands, wondering if I could see the spinning blood in my veins.

"But every strength can become a weakness. Your mother foolishly abused her magic."

"My mother was not a fool—" I said.

"An innocent fool," the witch said, cutting me off, "but she didn't understand the power of her transformations. She didn't realize they would rob her of her life. When she came to this mountain, she was nearly at her end. I found it a miracle that she lived long enough to marry and give birth to you."

"But why? What was so wrong with her spinning?"

"Well, surely you've guessed at the consequences of such magic," said the witch.

I thought for a moment. "Something to do with bargains?"

"A fair guess. When you gave your gold to the miller, you made a bargain, no?"

"A fool's bargain," said Red.

"Hush, girl."

Red was silent.

"He gave me food," I said.

"How much food?"

I hesitated. "Enough for me."

"But an even trade?"

I stood still. I knew it hadn't been an even trade, but I didn't want to believe our trades had been anything but normal. "The miller has *never* been fair. When has he ever made an even trade?"

"Spinning straw to gold is a dramatic transformation," said the witch. "It would take a lot out of a person, even their own control over their magic. You were unable to demand a fair bargain for your gold. You couldn't even name a price."

A chill ran through me. But that couldn't be true. "What about the king?" I said. "He took my gold and he didn't give me anything."

"Didn't he?"

I thought back to when King Barf had demanded the gold from me. I hadn't given it to him right away. I first asked him what he would give me. *Give me the gold and I will spare your life.* And I had given it to him.

"So . . . they can offer me *anything*? What if they offer me dirt, or a slug, or . . . or . . . something really awful?"

"Well, I suppose it could be awful. But so long as what they promise has some value and they are able to give it, then the bargain stands."

"What if I don't want what they offer?"

"Ah. That's what makes this a dangerous business. Your mother never would have come to me had she been able to refuse a bargain. That is the reason she came to me. When an offer was made, she was bound. She had to give them the gold, and she had to take what they offered, even if she didn't want it."

My will. My control. That was the price, the consequence, of this magic.

I thought of all those times I had brought gold to the miller. "What will you give me?" I had asked, so desperately, as if I were offering rubbish instead of gold. I had never made demands or requests. I had never refused his offer, and I hadn't even had the sense to question or wonder.

The magic had been working on me all this time, wrapping me up in tight tangles, robbing me of my control. I thought of my mother, drowning in all that gold.

"Couldn't you have helped my mother at all?"

"Well, I believe I *did* help her, though not in the way she expected."

"But she's dead!" Anger flared inside me like a hot spark. "If you really helped her, she wouldn't be dead!"

"Her fate was sealed long before she came to me," said the witch. "But while she was still alive, I told her of the one thing that could free her from her bindings."

"What?" I asked, feeling a speck of hope.

"Have you ever heard of a stiltskin?"

*Stiltskin.* It had a familiar sound, but I didn't know what it meant or where I might have heard it.

"A stiltskin is magic at its greatest. Pure magic, un-meddled-with and more powerful than any enchantment or spell."

"Where can I get one? What do they look like?"

"Well . . . they could be anywhere, I suppose, and they can look like anything. It could be a tree or a rock or a mountain. A stiltskin's magic grows with the object, becomes part of it. It's a real deep-in-the-bones kind of magic. It can't be taken away or undone or even abused. It's stronger than even the strongest curse. I told your mother that was the only way to untangle her mess. But she never did find one. At least not until it was too late."

"Then she did find one? Where is it? Do you have it?"

The witch looked startled, but then she smiled. "It is a good question, but the better question is, do you have one?"

"How could I? I've never heard of a stiltskin until now."

"Well, then, a stiltskin is something that must be found on one's own. It can't be borrowed or stolen. It has to be yours."

"How do I get one that's mine?"

"Well . . ." The witch paused, and I waited, certain she was about to tell me some great mystery, a secret that would make everything clear. But all she said was, "You have to look."

Witches are absolutely no help at all.

"What about her family? Did my mother tell you about her family in Yonder? Do they spin too?"

"Likely they do. She mentioned some sisters but never went into any great detail, not even whether they knew of her troubles. She may have run away before they found out."

"But they *could* know," I said. If I found my mother's family, they might be able to help me.

Help. I suddenly remembered the real reason I had come.

"Opal," I said. "The miller's daughter. I have to help her."

Red snorted. "Help her? You mean spin all the straw into gold for her?"

"Shouldn't I?"

"Rump, don't you understand what Granny was just explaining about the spinning and the bargains? What if Opal promises something really foolish?"

"How bad can it be? She wouldn't offer something too horrible."

"Strange promises can come out of the desperate," said the witch. "Sometimes it's best to leave others' destinies alone."

"And what of my own destiny?" I asked.

The witch's bright gaze pierced me right through. "It's yours to find, along with your name," she said.

"It's getting dark," said Red. "We have to go now. Mother will worry."

Gran would have been worried too. I wished she were here to worry over me.

We made to leave until the witch said, "Wait." I turned around. She came forward with her hand in a fist. "Hold out your hand." She reached out, and for a moment, I thought she was going to give me something special, maybe something magical that would help me. She dropped a speck in my hand, and all my hope drained away.

"Oh . . . Thank you. . . ." A seed. She had given me a tiny seed. What good would a seed do me in a mountain that refused to grow anything but pine trees and wild shrubs?

"Little things can grow big," she said.

I put the seed in my pocket and nodded, too exhausted to argue.

"One last thing," the witch said. "Watch your step."

Red and I walked in the snow, the stones on either side the only sign of the path. We didn't talk the whole way home. We were both thinking, though, and probably about the same things, but in different ways. I was thinking that I should help Opal. Red was thinking that I shouldn't. I was thinking about bargains and death. Red was thinking I was an idiot.

My thoughts turned again to my name and my destiny. Maybe there was more to it than I really knew. I felt it, as if it were hovering just above me but I couldn't grasp it. I did have a whole name. My mother had whispered it in my ear, and somewhere in the world it existed or I wouldn't be here. That's what I thought, anyway. But for now I wondered if the destiny I was following was connected to my real name or only the bit of the name I knew.

Just as we approached my cottage, I stepped into a ditch and went sprawling.

So much for heeding good advice.

# CHAPTER FOURTEEN

## Rump to the Rescue

It was afternoon when we reached my cottage. Red stood by me and finally spoke her mind.

"You're going to go, aren't you? To help Opal." It wasn't a question, really, and the declaration cleared my own doubt. I had to go.

Red let out a heavy sigh. Her brow was knit and her mouth curved down, but she didn't look angry. Was she sad? I'd never seen Red sad. That's when I realized that, even if she did call me an idiot, Red really cared what happened to me. She was my one true friend.

"Will you take care of Milk for me? She gives some milk still."

She nodded. "What about your donkey?"

"I'm taking him with me." I didn't want to burden Red too much, and even though Nothing was ornery and stubborn, he might be able to carry me or my things, if I could get him to move.

"How will you find Opal?" Red asked.

I shrugged.

"What if she's locked up?"

I shrugged.

"What if you get caught and shot with an arrow, or poisoned, or—"

"Then I'll be dead, Red." I smiled because of the rhyme, even though it wasn't a happy one.

Red gave me one of her rare smiles. "You're an idiot, Rump, but the smartest idiot I know."

I put my hands in my pockets, pulled out the seed Red's granny had given me, and held it up to the sun. I thought how the odds were stacked against both the little seed and me, a boy all tangled in life and magic. We didn't have a chance, really, but sometimes you still have to try.

"Little things can grow big," I said.

"Under the right circumstances," said Red, and she bent down and dug up some cold earth. I placed the little seed in the hole, and we covered it up.

After Red left, I stuffed just a few things in a satchel: a dry loaf of bread, some biscuits, a skin of water, and my mother's bobbin from her spinning wheel. I knew that it wasn't the reason for the magic, but I wanted it with me. A little piece of Mother, a piece of home. I wished I could take a piece of Gran with me too, but there was nothing. I would have to carry a memory.

It was late afternoon as I walked through The Village,

toward the road that led down The Mountain. I stopped once and looked back on The Village. I had never seen it from this view. The houses were stacked in jumbled clusters up the mountainside, some so lopsided they looked like they might slide right down. Smoke rose from chimneys, and windows were lit with candles. The mill stood above all the houses, the biggest building by far. High above the village were the mines that I had worked in my whole life. I had never been anywhere but this village. Even though I knew there were other kingdoms and villages and probably mountains all over the world, *this* had always been *my* world. I imagined my mother leaving Yonder and feeling the same.

In my mind I thought I would not be gone for very long, but in my heart I felt like I was leaving on a great expedition, and if I ever returned, I would be very different. I hoped I would be different.

I was leaving The Mountain at last. True, my leaving might have sounded far grander if I were leaving a place with a real name, like Ochenleff or Asteria. But I left just the same.

It all sounded so big and adventurous, but my lofty sentiments were squashed before I had gotten even halfway down The Mountain. Nothing didn't carry a thing. Instead, I hauled *him*. It was about as fun as playing with pixies. When I tried to ride him, he either wouldn't move or moved so fast I couldn't hold on. Then he stumbled and I fell off. I ended up pulling him the whole way while he bellowed and spit in my ear.

When I finally reached the bottom of The Mountain, it was night. Luckily, there was a little moonlight or I wouldn't have been able to see at all. I met a man driving a wagon and asked him how far it was to The Kingdom and what direction.

He pointed in the direction I was already going and said it was a good twelve miles. My heart sank. "I would gladly give you a ride in my cart," said the man, "but your donkey doesn't look like he'd keep up with the horse."

"No," I said, "he wouldn't." I wanted to kick Nothing. Maybe I could just tie him up here and get a ride anyway, but then someone might steal him. Worthless as he was, he was the only company I had on this journey. I gave another tug and we plodded down the road.

After an hour I was starving, so I ate all the biscuits in my sack. We found a stream to drink from and some early spring grass for Nothing. After that he settled right down in the grass and didn't want to move. I pulled and pulled, but he just bellowed. I got on his back and kicked him as hard as I could with both legs. He still didn't move. I pulled out my mother's bobbin and poked his side with it. He bellowed and jumped right up and started trotting down the path, with me hanging on him sideways.

Nothing carried me for only a few miles before I had to start pulling him again, and after another hour I wondered if the man with the cart had been mistaken and it was really twenty miles, or even thirty. I had no sense for distance. Maybe I wouldn't get there by tonight and something really awful would happen in the morning. What would the king do to Opal and her family if she didn't spin the straw into gold? How could I go back home if I failed?

The road widened and small houses started to appear, their windows all dark and quiet. It must have been very late, but the houses gave me hope that I was close to The King's City. The houses got closer together and smaller, then very close and stacked on top of each other. They looked like little towers made of rubble that a wind might blow over. Then they spread out a little and got bigger. A lot bigger. The road began to wind and curve up a steep hill, and at the top was a giant stone wall. Beyond that wall was King Barf's castle. Opal was there.

Nothing would not go up the hill. It was almost as steep as The Mountain, and no matter how much I poked and jerked and kicked, he wouldn't budge. So I reasoned that if he wouldn't budge for me, he wouldn't budge for anyone else, either. I left him on the side of the road, by a tree. And I hoped a swarm of pixies would bite his bony stubborn rump!

Halfway up the hill, my courage started to drain with my energy. In all the excitement of being a hero, I hadn't thought any of this through. When I started my journey, it was as if all the obstacles in my way weren't really obstacles at all—just minor annoyances. But when I reached the top of the hill, I realized that they were definitely obstacles—and big ones. The castle was surrounded by towering walls with closed gates, and soldiers guarding those gates with spears and bows and arrows.

Would I be a coward if I went back down the hill? What would Gran do? It was a silly question. Gran would never have gotten into this mess in the first place. Oh, how I wished I could talk to her now!

I needed to think.

I thought about what was in my way, and what I had to do to get it out of my way. I needed to get to Opal in the castle, but in my way there were guards and spears and arrows and a stone wall and possibly more of that beyond the wall. What did I have?

An ornery donkey stuck at the bottom of the hill, a dry loaf of bread, and an old bobbin. And one more thing. At that very moment, a miracle happened.

A horse and cart came up the hill, and the driver hopped down to speak with the guards.

"Straw deliveries go to the stables," said one of the guards. "Other side of the castle."

"This 'ere straw ain't for no stables. This is for a chamber. Had an order for it to be brought this way."

"Tonight?"

"I've got a letter."

Straw for a chamber! That had to be for Opal! The guard looked down at the letter the man was holding out. While they spoke, I crept to the back of the cart, unseen by the guards or the driver. I pulled myself up and dug myself into the straw until I was completely hidden. In a moment I heard the gates squeak open and the cart rolled forward. I almost laughed.

The cart ambled on for a minute but then stopped, and I heard the driver unhitch the mule. The driver spoke with probably more guards, and then I was pretty sure we were inside the castle because everything started to echo.

The straw was scratching at my arms and neck and everywhere. I struggled to remain still, and the itching stirred up an uncomfortable memory also involving straw. It had happened a few years ago. I was hiding from Frederick and Bruno in a barn behind a huge stack of straw. They were mad at me because I had sneezed really loudly in the middle of their older brother's wedding—right at the quiet part. So Frederick and Bruno were chasing after me, trying to light my pants on fire. I guess I should have realized that a haystack is not a smart place to hide when you're running from fire. The whole barn burned down and I barely made it out alive. Needless to say, my pants did catch on fire. The memory made me shudder. I suddenly wondered that I'd jumped into this pile of straw so readily.

Finally the cart stopped and the man knocked on a door. A few muffled exchanges. I heard a woman's voice, Opal's maybe. Suddenly I was tumbling out of the cart, rolling in the straw as it came down. The straw still covered me on the floor, and I heard the cart trundle away as the door shut.

I was just about to peek when I felt hands digging into the straw, pulling out big clumps. I froze and then someone grabbed my hair and yanked. I yelped and flopped out of the straw, hitting my head on the floor with a loud crack.

"Oh!" said a voice. I looked up and saw a woman standing over me. But it was not Opal.

The woman had a feather duster and a rag tucked in her skirt. She was older but tried to hide it with lots of rouge on her cheeks and lips. She was holding a big piece of fabric in one hand and a fistful of straw in the other.

This straw was to stuff a mattress. It wasn't for spinning.

The maid's surprised face suddenly turned hard. She scooted back and reached for something behind her, a poker, and pointed it right at me. "Get out, you little rascal. There's nothing in here for you to steal."

"I wasn't—"

She whacked me on the shoulder with the poker. "Get out!" She whacked me again. "You filthy mongrel, get out!" I scrambled to my feet, my satchel clutched to me. I tried to reach for the door, but the woman swung at me again and I rolled to the other side of the room.

"Thief!" the woman shrieked. "Thief!" I ducked as she jabbed at me again. "Thief in the castle!"

She lunged with the poker until I was pressed up against a window. A *window*! I hadn't gone up any stairs, so the ground must be just below. I fumbled behind me until I found a latch. The window flew open and I tumbled out, landing flat on my back. All the air was knocked out of me and sparks flew in my eyes, but I had to run because the maid's bellowing was sure to bring the guards after me any moment.

I ran along the castle walls until I found some bushes to hide in, then dove in. *Aargh!* They were full of thorns! I held still and didn't breathe. Thorns stuck in me everywhere, but I bit down on my tongue and watched as guards came to the window I'd fallen out of. A few jumped out and walked around, searching. One came to the very bush I was hiding in, but it was so dark and I was so still, he didn't see me. Soon, they were all gone.

I forced myself to wait in the bush a little longer, and while I did, all my pains sank in. My head and back were sore from the fall, and my shoulders stung from the maid's whacks. I had needle thorns sticking in my head and arms, but most especially in my bottom. Destiny can be so cruel.

I looked to the sky, wondering how long before dawn. The sky was still dark, but there couldn't be more than a few hours left, maybe even less. How much straw had the king given Opal to spin? And how long did she have to spin it? I'd better find her fast.

Slowly, I crept out of the bush and tried to remove all the thorns. The earth was wet and squishy beneath my feet, so my steps made squelching sounds. I froze and waited for movement or noise. All was still. Heroic rescues are not as glamorous as people imagine, I thought as I squished along in the muck.

The next step was to find a tower—I was sure Opal would be locked up in one. In Gran's stories, damsels in distress were always trapped in towers. That was the point of towers, so no one could rescue you unless your hair was a mile long. Opal's hair wasn't that long, so how to get in?

There were many towers in the castle. Which tower? *Think, think.* Most of the windows were dark, but two towers had lights in them that I could see. I considered the location of each tower. They were on opposite ends of the castle. On one end was the main gate to the castle, where the king and queen and other royal guests made their grand entrances. On the other end were the stables and blacksmith, where there were piles and piles of straw. If you needed to fill a room with straw, it would be better if the room were *near* the straw.

I approached the tower on the stable side. There was no one around, not even guards, which seemed odd. I put my hands on the tower wall, feeling around. A few stones budged. I could fit my hands easily in the cracks. I pulled one stone completely out. You'd think someone as rich as King Barf would keep his castle in better repair, there were so many holes and loose stones. But I suppose King Barf didn't worry much about the outside of his castle. He probably paid more attention to the inside, where all the gold was.

I started to climb. It wasn't so difficult, almost like climbing a tree. I just had to test each hold to make sure it would support my weight. Being small and skinny was really working in my favor. If I were a hulking, armor-clad hero, the tower would have crumbled like dry bread.

Tired and out of breath, I finally reached the window. Mercifully, it was open. I heard whimpering, and sniffling. Someone was crying. It had to be Opal. With the last of my strength, I pulled myself up, slid over the windowsill, and flopped on the ground like a giant slug.

"Oh!" Opal rushed to the fireplace and grabbed the poker. She stood over me, the poker raised over her head. I flinched. Opal lowered her weapon and stared at me with her big blue eyes. "What are you doing here?"

"I'm here to rescue you," I said.

She stared at me blankly, so blankly I thought maybe she hadn't heard me, and then she laughed. She laughed and laughed, high and shrill, and finally she snorted.

"Aren't you the one called Butt?"

It wasn't exactly the heroic welcome I'd hoped for.

"Rump," I said. "They call me Rump."

"Rump," she said, holding back a laugh. "Rump, my hero." Then she burst into more laughter. She leaned over, holding her stomach. She hee-hee-ed and ha-ha-ed and giggle-gaggled and fell into the straw, rolling in it like one of her brothers. And then suddenly she was crying. Not just whimper, whimper, sniffle, snuffle crying. Her whole body heaved with sobs and snot ran down her face and she didn't even bother to wipe it off.

"Hel-elp m-m-me? Y-you?" she sobbed. "I'm supposed to turn all this straw into gold because my f-father told the king I c-could!" I was getting nervous about all the noise she was making. What if someone came into the room to see if she was all right? Opal sobbed again, "Why did he do that?"

"Because I *can* spin the straw into gold," I said. "Your father knows I can. I think that's why he told the king. He didn't think he would take you away. He thought the king would just ask for more gold."

Opal stopped crying and wiped the snot from her nose on her sleeve. "Y-you? Th-the gold? You can spin the gold?"

I was surprised that she was so surprised. Had she never seen the gold before? Hadn't she wondered what I'd been trading for food all these months?

"Yes. I can spin the gold."

Opal wrinkled her nose as if I smelled rancid.

"Prove it. Spin all *that* to gold." She pointed to the heaping pile of straw in the corner. It was more than I had ever spun at once, maybe three or four mattresses full. In front of it was a spinning wheel, big and shiny, the wood freshly carved and polished.

"Well?" said Opal. She was tapping her foot impatiently. "What are you waiting for?" She didn't look so sweet or innocent anymore.

I sat down at the wheel and took a few straws in my hand. I could see things through Opal's eyes now, how ridiculous this seemed. *Me* spin straw into gold? How could a small, foolish boy possibly do such a thing? I had thought myself a great hero, but now I saw how silly I looked. With shaking hands, I fed the straw through the wheel and spun, holding my breath, ready for it to break and fall to the ground, just to mock me.

*Whir, whir, whir.*

Gold wrapped onto the bobbin. I released my breath.

Opal gasped and clapped her hands to her mouth. Her eyes showed that same greedy gleam I knew so well from the miller. She reached to touch the gold, but my hand came down over the bobbin.

"What will you give me?" I asked.

"Give you? I have to give you something?"

"You want me to spin a pile of straw into gold for nothing?"

"What do you want?"

I thought of all the things I wanted—more food on

The Mountain, a horse to replace Nothing, more hens, a family, my whole name. But the mere thought of asking for anything made my tongue swell and my mouth clamp shut. Just as the witch had said, I could make no requests, only beg and take what was offered. "What will you give me?" I asked.

Opal wound her tongue around her mouth, eyes blank. She put her finger to her lips and then her hands on her waist. Oh, bother, what was going through her mind? I was beginning to suspect that the name *Opal* bestowed a destiny that gave you lots of looks but maybe not so many brains.

Finally, she felt at her neck. "I will give you my necklace," she said, and relief washed over me once again. "My father gave it to me, and it's made of pure gold."

Probably gold I spun. I took the necklace and stuffed it in my pocket, breathing deeply. That wasn't so bad.

"Shut the windows," I said, getting down to business. They were still gaping open from my arrival.

"I like the fresh air. This straw makes me sneeze."

"I'm going to make a pile of *gold.* Every pixie within a mile of here will be swarming this room if you leave those windows open, and that will probably be worse than a sneeze."

She scowled at me and shut the windows. I began to spin again.

*Whir, whir, whir.*

Bit by bit, I worked on the pile of straw. As it dwindled, a stack of gold took its place. Opal watched, transfixed for a while, and then fell asleep on the floor, a skein of gold clutched in her hands.

I spun the last of the straw just as the sky turned purple. I crawled out the window, my eyes so heavy and my limbs so tired, I had to concentrate extra hard just to make my fingers grip the wall.

I had done my duty and now I could go home, but first I needed to eat and rest a little. I made my way across the castle grounds to the stables, where I ate the rest of the bread from my satchel. I was so thirsty I drank water from a horse's trough. The horse didn't seem to mind. Then I found an empty stall and made myself a nest of straw. I was becoming quite fond of straw. It's comfortable to sleep in and pixies don't like it. *Straw is better than gold,* I thought.

Just as I was drifting to sleep, I swore to myself that I would never spin again. Never. And I didn't want to look at gold ever again. But I was very tired, and I wasn't thinking clearly.

# CHAPTER FIFTEEN

## Straw, Straw, Straw

I woke to the sound of horses braying and geese honking. When I opened my eyes, I found I was in a dangerous position. A horse's rear end loomed right above my head.

People shouted back and forth, opening stalls, grabbing buckets and ropes. Someone came to my stall and removed the horse, which was a great relief, but then another person came and stuck a pitchfork into the pile of straw, narrowly missing my eye. I squeaked and quickly covered my mouth. The servant muttered something about rats and left.

I didn't know what to do. If I walked out of the stables, would someone stop me? Were they still searching for the thief from the night before? I decided that it would be better for me to stay still until things were quiet, maybe until dark even, and then I could go home.

I waited. I counted bits of straw, guessed how much

gold it could all make. I wished for food. I wasn't used to being hungry for very long anymore, since I had been trading the miller for food whenever I wanted. I was so hungry I sucked on bits of straw, and then I was dying of thirst. My mouth was hot and woolly, so I drank from the horse's trough again.

It's difficult to tell how much time is really passing when you're hungry and bored. They say that a minute is a minute no matter where you are or what you're doing, but my brain could never grasp that. I think time is a trickster. When I have a lot to do, time shrinks, but when I want something over with, it stretches and yawns, and laughs at my torture. Sometimes the minutes hold hours inside of them. This was one of those times.

I fidgeted and worried. I wondered what had happened to Opal. Had the king come for the gold? Would Opal go home then?

Finally, the setting sun, reddish orange, was filtering through the stable. The stable was loud and busy again, with servants unsaddling horses, feeding and brushing them. They all chattered idle gossip loudly. I was bored by what seemed so interesting to them. Lord So-and-So is to marry Lady Such-and-Such. A maid spilled a glass of wine on somebody. Baron Something-or-Other is raving again about trolls in The Eastern Woods.

"Come help me with the straw. The king wants it all in the west tower." A pitchfork plunged into my pile of straw.

"What for? We just put new straw in the beds."

"Don't know. He wanted a pile of it in there last night,

and now he wants all the straw from the stables up in the west tower, every last bit." Their pitchforks jabbed into the straw one after the other, and I had to shift and twitch so I wouldn't be stabbed.

"Is the king weaving baskets?"

The servants laughed. They filled a cart full of straw and left. Luckily, they didn't notice my head sticking above the rest of the pile.

I hid behind some large pails until it was dark and quiet. I was shaking. I couldn't go home. Not now that I knew Opal was still in trouble. Oh, I almost wished I hadn't overheard them talking! But why was I surprised? Why hadn't I thought of this? Last night was merely a test. Of course King Barf would order more straw, all the straw he had, and make Opal spin him more gold. But even then, would he be satisfied? Would he ever stop demanding more?

I didn't want to answer these questions about the future. I had to think about now. Opal was still in trouble, and it was more my fault than ever. I couldn't just leave her.

It was back up the tower for me.

When I plopped through the window this time, Opal seemed expectant. "Oh, I knew you would come, Robert!"

Robert? "It's Rump," I said.

"Oh, never mind that. I know Frederick and Bruno call you silly names. But I won't. I shall call you Robert. A proper name." She smiled as if that were the kindest thing in the world, but I couldn't smile back. I was gazing openmouthed at all the straw. There was twice, no, three times as much straw as before, all piled along the walls and halfway up to the ceiling.

"Troll's breath," I muttered.

"Oh, it's not so bad, is it?" said Opal. "You can spin this in a wink, you're so clever."

I felt ill and must have looked it. Opal's eyes brimmed with tears and her chin quivered as she spoke. "You must! The king says if every last straw isn't gold by morning, I'm going to die! They're going to k-kill me!" And she wailed, though I didn't think it was quite as sincere as the night before. There wasn't any snot. But sincere or not, what choice did I have?

"What will you give me?" I asked.

Opal folded her lower lip down so that she looked like a large toddler on the verge of a tantrum. "I already gave you my necklace. That was made of pure gold, you half-wit! Do you realize how much that's worth?"

"That was for last night. You have to give me something for tonight, and besides, I'm making you a *mountain* of pure gold," I said impatiently. Who was the half-wit here?

Opal looked around desperately. It made me nervous to watch her think. She looked so blank and mystified. She brushed her hands down her hair, licked her lips again, fiddled with her dress, and finally fumbled with her fingers.

"I will give you my ring," she said as she pulled a little ring off her finger. It was not gold or silver, probably cheap tin, but it had a small stone in the middle, shiny white with swirls of purple and blue. An opal.

"My mother gave it to me," she said, "before she died." She dropped it in my hand, and I felt a stab of guilt. I didn't think there was anything she could give or promise me that would be worth more than a hulking pile of gold, but I could see this was probably close, a priceless token. I was starting to really dislike this whole binding bargains and promises thing. Still, it wasn't anything horrible.

"Close the windows," I said, and started to spin. My limbs still ached from the previous night's work. My leg pulsed with pain every time it pushed down on the treadle. But I kept going.

*Whir, whir, whir.* Gold, gold, and more gold. I had searched for it my entire life, and here it was, pouring out like water. I hated the sight of it.

Opal fell asleep faster this time, one hand twined in the gold, the other clutching some straw. As the first rays of morning light reached the sky, I grasped the straws from her hand and spun them too. The gold was piled all around me now, and to me it just looked like heaps of shiny straw. I didn't see why people loved it so much.

Just as I was descending the tower, the door unlatched and King Barf said in his nasally drawl, "Ah, my sweet girl, you are a treasure beyond compare."

My fingers were stiff and sore. My leg was cramped, and my back and head ached. Climbing down the tower was agony, but all I could think of was going home. Home and food. My stomach rumbled as I touched the ground, but then I heard another rumbling. It was growing louder, and it was definitely not my stomach.

I stood in the middle of the castle grounds, not

bothering to hide myself. I couldn't move and I couldn't speak, even though my mouth hung wide and my tongue wagged. I started to drool.

A procession of wagons rolled through the gates and up to the doors of the castle. One, two, three . . . more than a dozen cottage-sized wagons.

Wagons stacked high with straw.

I sat against a tree and watched as the servants unloaded the straw, bundled it up, and hauled it inside. With each bundle they carried in, I felt weight pressing down on me, heavy as gold. I had a hard time breathing, and I realized what should have been obvious to me from the beginning. This was my destiny—to spin gold at the whims of a greedy king for the rest of my life.

I thought that when you found your destiny, you were supposed to be happy about it. But maybe I was wrong. Maybe it was something you just had to accept. Succumb to. Hadn't I seen the villagers on The Mountain succumb to their fates all my life? They accepted it because they had always known their name and the destiny that came with it. And they knew those things couldn't be changed. Maybe I just needed to accept what was in front of me.

I felt very heavy and sleepy. There was so much spinning to do. I should go right back to Opal now, but I needed to close my eyes just for a little while. I moved in the direction of the stables, but someone stopped me. "Ho there, boy, where are you going?"

"To the stables," I said sleepily. I didn't care what he thought.

"Not now, lad, we've got work to do," and he dropped

a bundle of straw at my feet. "Take it inside and follow the rest." I looked up and saw a procession of people carrying straw on their backs into the castle.

With a deep breath, I swung the straw onto my back. My knees buckled under the weight. I followed the line, into the castle, up some stairs, and into a chamber. We must have been in a different tower, because this room was three times the size of the last one. The straw was piling up in the corners and crawling up the walls, covering the tapestries, the paintings, and the windows. This would never stop. As long as there was straw in The Kingdom, King Barf would want it spun into gold.

I fell helplessly into the straw and buried myself under it. No one noticed me as the workers piled straw higher and higher until it covered the windows and all the light was shut out.

# CHAPTER SIXTEEN

## One Bargain Too Many

I woke with a start. How long had I slept?

Someone was sobbing. Was I too late? I dug through the straw until I rolled out of the pile and onto the floor at Opal's feet. Opal squealed. Her face was red and wet, but it got redder, and her sad eyes narrowed to angry slits.

"Where have you been?!" Opal demanded, hands on her hips.

"Unloading straw."

Piles of straw reached nearly to the ceiling. They were stacked right up against the fireplace, where flames snapped precariously. Opal stood between the fireplace and the spinning wheel.

"Well, just look at this room," she said, as if she were my mother and scolding me for not picking it up.

"Lots of straw," I said.

"Exactly! The king has promised to make me queen after this batch, and if you mess it up, you'll be the first person I behead!"

I was going to say that if I messed it up, she wouldn't be queen to behead anyone, but I was too tired to argue. My only comfort was that if I messed up, Opal and the miller would be punished too. I imagined them both chained in a dungeon.

I sagged into the wheel and piled straw on my lap. The window was covered by straw, so I couldn't see if it was still light out or if night had fallen. It had been early morning when I fell asleep, but there was so much straw. No matter what time it was, I needed to work fast. I took a deep breath and twisted the straw into the wheel and pressed my foot on the treadle. All the aches and cramps returned.

I spun as fast as I could, and Opal paced in a little circle, rubbing her hands together impatiently. "Can't you spin any faster?"

"No."

"Keep the straw close to you! Don't let it spill!" She snatched some of the straw that had fallen from my lap and threw it on my head. "Don't you know what will happen if every last bit isn't turned to gold by morning? No wonder my brothers say you're a numbskull."

I stopped spinning. "Would you like to continue?"

Opal pressed her lips together and glared. "Keep spinning, or else . . ."

Or else we were both dead. I worked faster than ever. I piled the straw on top of me and worked the treadle as if I were pumping in order to breathe.

Hours passed. My whole body felt like one big cramp from sitting at odd angles and spinning for so long. Despite the growing pile of gold, the straw loomed over me like a beast prepared to swallow me whole.

I worked faster. Soon I could see the tapestries on the walls. Then the windows. It was dark out, which meant there was still time.

The sky began to lighten as I was coming close to finishing. The walls were now stacked with skeins of gold. I kept an open space between me and the window so I could leave. I just hoped these walls were as easy to climb as the other tower.

Only a few handfuls of straw remained at my feet. Opal had fallen asleep by the fire, her head resting on a pile of gold. A string of slobber hung from her mouth. The fingers of one hand were clasped around a finger on her other hand, as if she were missing something there. Her ring.

I stopped spinning.

I hadn't made Opal give me something. I'd been so concerned with getting the spinning done in time that I forgot to ask. I had spun the gold, but what would happen if we didn't bargain? Would it turn back to straw? Would someone get hurt? Maybe I wouldn't be able to leave the castle.

"Opal," I whispered loudly. "Opal, wake up."

"Huh?" She sat up. Her face had big red marks on one side from the way she'd slept in the gold. Her hair was pushed up and ratted all funny. She smacked her lips and wiped the slobber from her mouth. "Are you done yet?" She yawned.

"Almost, but you forgot to give me something."

"You never asked," she said with an innocent smile.

"Well, I'm asking now. What will you give me?"

"Nothing," she said haughtily, like she already thought herself a queen. "You've almost finished spinning, and I have nothing left to give. I already gave you my two most valuable possessions." She still rubbed at her ring finger.

"Well," I said, spinning the last of the straw, "I can't let you have the gold unless you give me something. In fact, I can't even leave here until you give me something. Won't it be a surprise when the king comes in and finds me here, sitting at the spinning wheel?"

Her face scrunched up in anger, making her look wild and ugly. "Get off! Get away from that wheel!" she growled. "No one would believe a little numbskull like you could do it! This gold is mine!" She bent over to pick up a skein of gold, but couldn't. She tugged and pulled and scratched, but it was like the gold had all melded to the floor and hardened together. I let out a mirthless laugh. She couldn't take it! The magic wouldn't let her.

"What have you done?" she snarled. "You little scoundrel! I'll have your head for this!"

"The gold isn't yours," I said calmly. "You didn't give me something, so it's not yours. When the king comes, he won't be able to get it, either." I smiled. Magic is so clever and logical!

The wild look fell from Opal's face. She seemed to shrivel, and her tongue flicked out and wound around and around.

"Give you something," she muttered. She scratched at herself, pulled at her hair, yanked at her dress. Oh no, was she going to give me her dress?

"You don't have to give me a *thing*," I said desperately. "You could make me a promise to give me something later." I had no idea if that would work, but Opal was making me nervous, and suddenly the witch's warning was echoing in my brain. *Strange promises can come out of the desperate.*

"Promise you something?" She thought out loud. "Well, I'll be queen. I suppose I'll be able to give you most anything. But I can't give you gold, no, the king, my future husband, won't allow it. But what can I be sure I can give you? I don't know what my possessions will be."

I was getting impatient. The sun was spilling over the stables now. "Just promise me something. You can give me anything, anything you know is yours. I'm not asking for your firstborn child."

"My child? You want a child?"

"No, that's not what I—"

"Of course, you will probably never be able to have any of your own. And I might have more than I can care for." She was rambling to herself now. "My mother had ten children, and her mother had a dozen. I'm sure I shall be the same. What is wrong with giving one to someone who shall have none? Or if I never have one, I won't have to give it away. What harm is it to promise something that may never be?"

"Opal—" There were footsteps coming up the tower. I wanted to tell her it didn't need to be a baby. It could be a biscuit, it could be an apple, it could be her dress! But my tongue became a rock in my mouth. "Just give me something," I said. "What will you give me?"

The footsteps came closer, and Opal tensed. "Get out! Get out! You cannot be here when he comes!" She pushed me toward the window.

"What will you give me? You can't take the gold until you give me something!" I teetered on the windowsill.

Opal looked back at the door and at the gold all around her. Keys jingled in the lock.

"Opal!"

"I'll give you my firstborn child. I promise." She snatched a skein of gold and held it to her chest. She smiled triumphantly at me and stroked the gold as if it were a furry pet.

The door swung open.

I fell out the window.

That moment would have been a good time to have a pile of straw beneath me. But for all the straw I had dealt with in my life, there was not even a tiny bit when I needed it most. I hit the ground, bounced and rolled, and finally came to rest against a thorny shrub.

"Ouch," I croaked, and squeezed my eyes shut. Pain spread all over me and on me and in me. Thorn pricks and bruises and cuts and—

"Ouch!" It hurt to breathe. I think I broke my ribs and possibly my arm. I wasn't sure I could even feel my legs.

A flurry of movement and noise surrounded me, but everything was blurred and spinning.

"What's that?"

"He just fell from that tower!"

"Is he dead?"

"He's alive, I think."

Someone bent over me. "Are you alive?"

"I'm alive," I said breathlessly, "and I'm going to have a baby."

"What did he just say?"

"Something about a baby."

"A baby," I said, and then I blacked out.

# CHAPTER SEVENTEEN

## Martha's Endless Tales

"The king is going to marry tomorrow? A *commoner?*"

"It's what they're saying. A very rich commoner. Supposedly she can turn straw into gold. They say she's a witch."

A man and a woman were speaking in hushed but dramatic voices. I tried to open my eyes, but my lids were heavy.

"But the king wouldn't marry a witch!"

"He would if she could turn straw into gold. Nothin' the king loves more than gold, and I think he'd do anything to get it."

I felt like I was waking from a very bad dream where I had just been promised a baby, into another bad dream where my whole body felt like I had fallen out of a tower. Then I remembered that both were true. I groaned.

"Oh, he's waking! Poor thing."

I opened my eyes to see the woman leaning over me. She was very plump, and even though she seemed worried, I thought she must be a kind person. Her cheeks were round and red as apples, and all the lines in her face looked like they naturally moved upward into broad smiles and hearty laughs.

"Here now, little lamb," she said. "Drink up. There's a lad." She placed a cup to my mouth and I drank a hot broth. It helped me wake up a little and I looked around to see where I was.

The room was large and bustling. I hadn't noticed all the other noise, but servants were coming and going, bringing dishes and trays and buckets and rags. Two large fireplaces were burning bright with large pots over the flames. The walls were gray crumbling stone. I was in the kitchens of the castle. This was not where I wanted to be.

"You took quite a fall there, boy." A man came and stood beside me. He wore a red-and-gold uniform, with a big sword at his side. I shrank back. "Don't worry," he chuckled. "I'm not going to hurt you, though you were causing mischief, now, weren't you?" The guard didn't seem accusing; rather, amused. He was much younger than the kind woman, but he had the same laughing face, covered with a beard.

"Oh, Helmut, he's just a curious boy," said the woman, chuckling. "Remember how you were, now, always sneaking around corners, trying to get a peepsy at anything mysterious or exciting. I remember the time you pinched a swig of the king's finest wine when you were just a lad and it all came back up on my clean kitchen floor!"

"Yes, you whacked me a good one for that," said the soldier, "which is why I straightened out and became a keeper of the peace from little hooligans like—"

"He was only curious. No crime in that, now is there? Probably heard the gossip and came runnin' to see. I'm curious too. Mighta climbed the tower myself if I didn't think I'd bring down the whole castle." She chuckled and her whole plump body laughed with her, like Oswald the miller, only I liked her—and her laugh—much better. It made me want to laugh too, only instead of laughing, my body seized up in pain and I coughed my lungs out.

"Oh, now, there, there, little lamb, drink some more. You've banged yourself up quite a bit. There's no padding on those scrawny bones of yours. Can be quite useful, you know." She patted her wide hips.

"Now, then, what's your name? Everyone prefers to be called by their name, don't they?"

Not everyone.

"Robert," I said. The lie just slipped from my mouth, and I realized it was what Opal had called me. But I was glad I didn't tell her my real name. Everyone on The Mountain already knew, so I'd never had to explain it to anyone, and I didn't want to explain it now. I didn't have the energy.

"Well, Robert," said the woman, "I'm Martha, one of the king's cooks, and this is my son, Helmut. I named him so he could be a stalwart soldier, brave and fearless—"

"Which I am," said Helmut.

"But, really, he wouldn't hurt a fly. I might as well have named him Fluffy."

"That's enough, you old bat," said Helmut, but he was smiling.

"That's 'Mother' to you, Fluffy. Now give me those stockings."

Helmut held out a pair of stockings worn through with holes, and Martha began to darn them. It reminded me painfully of Gran. Gran used to darn my stockings. Now they had a lot of holes in them. I could feel my toes sticking out, rubbing against the worn leather of my shoes.

"Well," said Helmut, "I'd best get back to my post. Looks like we'll need to be extra vigilant to keep young hooligans from trying to get a peek at the future queen. The king has ordered a double guard around her chamber." He winked at me, then kissed his mother on the cheek and left. Martha looked after him as though she were very proud, even if she did tease him about his gentleness. I wondered if my mother ever would have looked at me like that, had she lived.

"Now, Robert," she said. I looked around a bit, wondering who she was talking to, until I remembered that *I* was Robert. "What brings you here? You don't belong in the castle, now, do you?" I froze, my mind racing to come up with some explanation, but Martha didn't wait for an answer. "Oh, don't tell me. I can tell it's a secret, and so you'd better keep it because I won't.

"Strange business, this girl and the gold. No good can come of it, if you ask me. I never saw anything good come of magic in the end, you know. Always a price to pay. I knew a woman who worked in the kitchens who went to a witch to get a potion to make her beautiful, and the potion did make her beautiful but it gave her horrible breath, so what good could it do? And she got old besides. There is no potion I know of for curing old age. Ah, me."

Martha talked without breathing, ten words for every stitch in the stocking, and she stitched fast, but I didn't mind, because it saved me from having to explain myself.

"Now, this business with the gold . . . If that King Bartholomew Archibald Reginald Fife is as wise as his name, which I seriously doubt, he'll keep away from this mischief and focus on crops. Gold won't feed a kingdom."

It wouldn't? On The Mountain, gold had always meant food. The miller Oswald said it himself. "Gold means food." And the more you found, the more you ate. But then I supposed the food had to come from somewhere. "Is there not much food in The Kingdom?" I asked Martha.

"Oh, goodness, didn't you know? But, no, you're so young, you can't be more than ten." This surprised me. Even though I was twelve, I'd never passed for eight. I was delighted to be pronounced ten.

"Well," continued Martha, "the crops in The Valley have suffered from bad weather and such. It's not a famine this year, but if we have another poor harvest . . . well, then, we can all add a little more water to our stew." So there really had been a shortage of food. Perhaps I had judged the miller Oswald too harshly.

"But the scarcity is everywhere," Martha continued. "We haven't had much gold come from The Mountain, and that is our main source of trade, you know. And gold is all the king cares about. Dear me, have you been in the castle? Gold everywhere. Not in the kitchens, of course, but everywhere else—gold mirrors, gold vases, even the floors are gilded with gold, and the king drapes himself in gold every day."

Martha continued stitching as she spoke. "He could probably trade the gold with another kingdom for some extra food, but oh no, it is the delight of his life. The servants spend half their time warding off pixies. Oh, dear me, what a nuisance. I know a wench who's swollen half the time from all the bites. But if that troubles the king, you'd never know it. And here we are on the brink of starvation." She sighed, the first breath I'd heard from her in ten minutes.

"Well, you can't neglect your crops and expect to feast. Maybe this girl will set us right in the end. Perhaps she can make gold into milk and potatoes."

Martha went on, speaking of different calamities magic had brought, and the gossip about the girl who could turn straw into gold. She knew all the details of the wedding that was to take place the next day, down to what flowers would go on the cake and in the bride's hair, and how the king was planning to throw out gold coins to the crowds.

Martha continued to talk as she bustled around the kitchen, chopping meat and vegetables. She fed me a delicious meat pie, and when I tried to get up, she pushed me back down and told me I wouldn't be moving that night. "But you tell me where to find your mother and I'll fetch a gnome to send her a message so she doesn't worry. You need to rest after such a fall."

"Well . . . I . . ."

"Oh, I see," she chuckled. "She doesn't know where you've gone. You are a mischievous little one. Well, I can't say my Helmut didn't do the same, always seemed to be up to his nose in trouble, but still she'll worry her heart out for you, so we must send a message. I'll say that you've had a bit of an accident. No need to give the details, but tell her you're safe and Martha will care for you until you're well enough to go home. Now what is your mother's name, dear?"

My tongue wagged. "Red," I blurted. If a message had to go to someone, it might as well go to her. That way I wouldn't have to explain anything to Martha.

"Strange name. She must be a curious person." I silently agreed. "But, then, I don't put much stock in names these days. I knew a girl named Gladiola who was supposed to be beautiful but she grew crooked and cross-eyed, and then there's my Helmut, ah, me." She laughed and moved to the window. "Message!" she said in a high, singsong voice, and she pulled up a fat little gnome who wriggled with excitement.

"Now, what would you like to tell her, Robert?"

"Uh . . . tell her I'm sorry to make her worry. I'll be home soon."

Martha spouted off a long message to the gnome, including all the details of my injuries, precisely where I was, and who Martha was and her son Helmut. When she asked the gnome to repeat the message, he got it all mixed up, and so she did it again and made it longer, but he still got it all mixed up, and so they went back and forth, and finally Martha lost patience and threw him out the window. The gnome scurried away chanting, "Red for message! Red for message!"

I wondered how long it would take him to find Red and if she'd make any sense of the message. She'd probably understand enough, and I knew what she'd think. She'd think that she had told me so.

I had spun myself a heap of trouble. Opal had promised me her firstborn child! My stomach was sick with the thought. Opal didn't understand the magic. She didn't think I would ever really take her baby, or perhaps she thought she could back out of her side of the bargain. But what she didn't understand was that I *had* to take the baby! Red had explained to me that rules are rules and the magic binds you to those rules. Opal had promised her baby. She had taken my gold. I must take her baby if she ever had one.

But that was only the beginning of my troubles. There was still the spinning and the gold. Surely the king would want Opal to spin more. Would he threaten to kill his own queen if she didn't spin more straw into gold? Would I have to stay here forever, always at the queen's beck and call when she needed straw spun to gold?

No. I couldn't.

I thought of all the things Opal could foolishly promise me. Her right eye. An arm and a leg. More children. I saw my destiny clearly now. I was holding a dozen crying babies and trying to spin a mountain of straw into gold while Opal screamed at me to hurry up because she's the queen. I felt dizzy. My head hurt. I couldn't go home. I had to get away, far away. I had to go someplace where I wouldn't hear about Opal or the king or a baby.

But mostly I had to find a stiltskin. A stiltskin was the only way to fix all this mess. That's what my mother had been looking for. That's what The Witch of The Woods said I needed.

But where could I find one? The witch said I must *look*, but look *where*? Under rocks? Under the ground? In a tree? In the sky? In Yonder or Beyond?

In the morning, the castle rang with chimes and bells, not like the single gong of the village bell in The Mountain, but dozens of them ringing in all different tones. It should have been a lovely sound, but it made my head throb and ache.

"Well, Robert," said Martha. "I'm off to the wedding. Methinks I shall fetch a bit of gold today. Wouldn't that be something? Be good and rest, and I shall bring you back a coin made by your very own queen. Maybe some good will come of it. There's bread and more pies, dear. Tuck in and eat, eat, eat! I hate to see such skinny bones on a growing boy."

When Martha was gone, I sat up and threw off the blankets. I slid out of bed, wincing at the pain in my sides. I felt dizzy on my feet and steadied myself for a moment. Martha had placed all my things neatly by the fire. My shoes and my little satchel with the bobbin and waterskin.

I ate another meat pie and a slice of bread, and because Martha had told me to eat, I put the loaf of bread in my satchel and another pie. I felt guilty, but I needed some food to travel. I wished I could do something for Martha for being so kind to me—spin her a spool of gold, or a pile of it—but for all her kindness, she hadn't made me any bargains. Besides, she didn't have a spinning wheel.

And, quite frankly, I was done with spinning. It was time to leave it all behind. Forever.

# CHAPTER EIGHTEEN

## In Search of a Stiltskin

Getting out of the castle was a lot simpler than getting in, especially with the wedding. I was practically flooded out by the parade of people flowing through the gates, shouting and throwing handfuls of grain. They must not be too worried about famine. But I suppose if you had a queen who could turn straw into gold, you wouldn't worry about much of anything.

The day was sunny and warm, perfect for a wedding. Gnomes skipped and pranced among the crowds, squealing the day's wonderful news.

> The king has wed! The king has wed,
> To the girl who spins the golden threads!

I followed the crowd down the hill, and who would have thought? Nothing was right where I'd left him, chewing grass and looking bored. I guess no one thought it worth their while to take him, or he wouldn't go even if they'd tried. I was actually a little proud of Nothing as I took hold of the rope and pulled him away.

Soon the royal carriage emerged from the castle gates behind me to parade through The Kingdom and display the new queen. The roads were flooded with nobles and soldiers and servants and peasants, and they all erupted into victorious shouts as the carriage came into view. There was Opal, *Queen* Opal, wearing a golden crown on her head and a gown embroidered with gold thread. She smiled but looked as blank as ever, and her tongue wound around her mouth. I wondered if she was still nervous.

King Barf's gold crown was bigger than his head, and he was dressed in even more gold than the first time I saw him. Gold breastplate, armbands, a gold-hilted sword and scabbard, gold tassels and buckles, and gold embroidery all over. It was amazing they both weren't devoured by pixies, but then I saw a dozen servants surrounding them, swatting the pixies away with big paddles or spraying them with dirt. The carriage was also encased in light netting.

A few unfortunate servants were tossing fat gold coins into the street, warding off the pixies as best they could. People were crawling and scratching to get at the gold. The miller and all his sons were in the crowd, and they bumped and shoved more than anyone, snarling to get the coins. It was like watching a pack of wild beasts fight over pieces of meat. Animals. That was all they were.

As I pushed my way out of the swelling crowd, I saw someone else I recognized. Kessler the peddler sat on the side of the road, all by himself. His patchy sack lay limp and empty by his side. He was barefoot and filthy, his bright orange hair dingy from dirt and grease. But at least he had no mice around him. I wondered how he'd gotten rid of them. Perhaps he could tell me how to undo all the trouble I had caused!

Kessler held a small object up close to his face. Then he pressed the object between his hands, closed his eyes, and muttered something. When he opened his hands and peeked inside, he growled with rage and frustration, and then repeated the ritual.

"Hello, Kessler," I said.

"What?" He looked around wildly to see who had spoken to him, and finally focused on me. "Oh yes, hello there. Fine day to you, sir." He looked back down at his hands and muttered some more. I leaned in closer to see what he held and caught a glint of gold. One of the fat gold coins from the wedding.

"What are you trying to do?"

"Multiply, multiply," he said, and scratched at his head. "More gold. More, more, more." He started muttering again and rubbed the coin between his hands.

"What happened to the mice? How did you make them go away?" I asked.

"What? Mice? Oh. They're gone. I can make things disappear, you know. Would you like to see? But, oh . . . I forgot, I forgot. What did I forget?" He scratched and pulled at his hair. Then he went back to his gold coin, holding it to his face and whispering to it.

I stared at him, horrified. Poor Kessler! He had been driven mad by his magic, yet he couldn't stop. Was this what was to become of me?

I pulled at Nothing and we turned down a road that led away from the crowds, and the king and queen, and Kessler.

I crossed a bridge over a river and came to a sign that pointed in the direction I was headed. It read:

## YONDER AND BEYOND

Yonder. Where my mother was from. Yonder was far from The King's City, and if her family was still there, perhaps they would know about the spinning and how I could get out of this heap of trouble. Maybe I could even learn my name.

We had barely traveled a mile when dusk approached. I wanted to get a little farther from The Kingdom, but Nothing kept turning around and going in the other direction. Then when I had him headed the right way, he kept stopping to graze the grass. We were moving so slowly that the ants beneath us reached a destination before we did. I made up a rhyme about Nothing:

*Nothing's a fool*
*He does nothing but drool*

> But I rule as fool
> 'Cause I stepped in his pool
> Of drool

It was getting dark in The Eastern Woods. I was exhausted even though we'd probably traveled only two miles after all of Nothing's walking in the wrong direction, and my whole body was still stiff and sore from my fall.

Then a gnome scurried up the road squealing, "Message for Rump! Message for Rump!" The gnome came right up to my feet. "Message for Rump! Message for Rump!"

"I'm Rump," I said, irritated.

The gnome jumped with glee, but he was breathing hard. He must have run a long time to catch up with me. Did these creatures ever lose energy? The gnome cleared his throat and got on with delivering his message, half shouting, half squealing.

> Dear Rump,
>
> You idiot. What did you do, fall out of a tower? We know Opal will be queen now, and Granny says if you keep spinning for her, it will come to no good—if it hasn't already. No more bargains. Get away from her as fast as you can and hide. Opal will have to deal on her own.
>
> Your friend,
> Red
>
> P.S. Granny told me to remind you: Watch your step.

Of course! Such useful advice after I'd already fallen out of a tower.

The gnome bounced eagerly in front of me, hoping to carry another message. I snatched him by the ears and held him up.

"Take this message back to Red."

Dear Red,
    I fell out of the tower because Opal promised to give me her firstborn child in exchange for the gold. What would you have done? I've already taken your advice to get as far away as possible. I'm traveling to Yonder, if I don't starve before I get there, or get eaten by pixies, or trolls, or annoyed to death by gnomes.
                    Your friend,
                    Rump

"Now repeat," I told the gnome.

The gnome repeated the message, even the part about the gnomes annoying me, with squealing excitement. It occurred to me that gnomes didn't really have brains, just some space in their heads that stored all our words and spat them back out when they reached the receiver. They could even insult themselves with glee.

The gnome scurried off screeching, "Message for Red! Message for Red!" I wondered if he would stop to sleep or eat before he got there. I knew I needed to eat and find a place to sleep. I had to stop for the night, and I couldn't rely on the hope that I might find a farm or a village soon.

The side of the road was thick with trees and shrubs. Maybe I could find some early berries, or some edible mushrooms, so I could save Martha's bread and pie for later. Who knew how long I would be on the road? I tugged at Nothing to go into the trees but he didn't move.

"There's better grazing in here," I said. I tugged some more but Nothing didn't budge. I slapped his rear and yanked and pulled, and then he drove forward and knocked me flat on my back. The wind whooshed out of me. I stuck my tongue out at Nothing and left him grazing in the road.

I walked into the trees a ways. It was early spring, so the plants were just starting to sprout and grow buds, but nothing was edible yet. I turned up leaves and dug a bit in the dirt, but I didn't find so much as a snail. I walked farther and suddenly, right before me, was the most amazing sight. An apple tree! A huge apple tree, its branches bent to the earth with the weight of apples. Ripe red juicy apples, beckoning me to sink my teeth into them.

My mouth watered. I stepped forward and reached for an apple.

*SNAP!*

*Schwip!*

*Schlunk!*

Instantly, I was seized by my ankle and yanked upside down into the air. I yelped and wriggled, but my ankle was held fast by some kind of rope. Next moment I heard something big lumbering through the brush.

"We've got one! We've got one!" A creature burst through the trees. "We've got . . . a boy?"

More creatures came rushing through the trees. They were all big and brutish with arms as thick as my stomach that hung down to their knees. Their faces were squashed and animal-like, with bulbous noses and yellow eyes and teeth.

Trolls!

# CHAPTER NINETEEN

## Trolls, Witches, and Poison Apples

The trolls heaved and grunted at the sight of me. They smacked their lips. "Well done, Brother. Looks like your trap caught us a nice, tasty boy."

"But I wanted a goat," said the first troll.

"Oh no, a boy is even better, much more succulent. Practically a feast." They all snorted and hopped up and down.

"He's awful skinny. Do you think his legs will have any meat?"

"I get the fingers. They look like the juiciest part of him."

"I'll take the rear. I've been longing for a rump roast."

I couldn't help it. I started laughing. Rump roast! My destiny was to be eaten!

"He laughed! I like this human. Let's eat him now." The trolls closed in on me and licked their lips with horribly long gray tongues. I twisted and writhed, trying to free myself. If I could just get down, I had a sliver of a chance of getting away, but it was no use. My bindings only tightened with my squirming, and the trolls were now packed in a circle around me. I squeezed my eyes shut and prepared for the worst.

"Wait!" said a troll. I opened my eyes. The troll held out his arms to stop the others from coming closer. Maybe he wanted to eat me all by himself. He sniffed hard through his fat, misshapen nose. "Do you smell that?" The other trolls sniffed too and stalked forward, until they were all right up close. From upside down, I could see straight up their noses, all hairy and slimy.

"He smells . . . ," said one troll.

". . . not like most humans," finished another.

"Cut him down," said the first troll. "And don't let him go."

It was hard to tell from upside down, but I thought the trolls looked a little confused.

With a quick slash, I was released and fell right at the feet of my captor. I looked up at him and squealed. He was terrifyingly ugly and smelled even worse. "Bring him over near the fire," he told the others. "Mard will want to see this."

The fire. They didn't want to eat me cold. The trolls dragged me through the trees like a dead rabbit. I couldn't speak or even move.

"Scared out of his senses," laughed one troll.

"We have that effect on humans."

The trolls dragged my limp body farther into the trees

until we reached a small clearing where there was a large fire and even more trolls sitting around it. They released me and I scrambled to my hands and knees to search for a way to escape, but I was surrounded. Surrounded by smelly, ugly, man-eating trolls. A pot of some stinking brew was boiling over a fire. Maybe they intended to cook me in that.

"What's this?" said a girl troll. The only reason I thought she was a girl was because her voice was slightly higher and she had two long, tangled braids. Otherwise, she looked the same as the rest.

"This boy tried to eat the apples," said the troll dragging me.

"Of course he did," said the girl troll. "But what did you bring him here for?"

"Bork did it," said one. "He said to not let him go!"

The first troll, the one they called Bork, reached down and lifted me up by the back of my shirt with one hand. I flailed my arms as I hung in the air. "Smell 'im, Mard," said Bork.

The girl troll bent down and sniffed a little, and then a lot. I held my breath so I wouldn't have to sniff her. Finally, her eyes widened and she looked up at Bork.

"Strange," said the girl troll. I guessed her name was Mard.

"I know," said Bork. "I almost wish he had eaten one of those apples, just to see what would've happened."

A few trolls growled at Bork. They all seemed to think he had said something really horrible. A few of the trolls closed in on me. Maybe they thought the apples would spoil the taste of their dinner. All this talk of food was making me hungry, and if I couldn't eat before I died, I'd like to die quickly. "Could we get this over with, please?" I said.

The trolls looked at me, confused. I guess they didn't often have people begging to be eaten.

"Get what over with?" said one. "Who do you think you are, making demands?"

"Well, I've been through a lot and I could use a break. So if you could just eat me fast . . ."

The trolls were all silent for a moment as they looked from each other to me and back to each other. Then they all started laughing, or I guessed they were laughing. Their bodies were heaving like laughter, but the laughs sounded more like growls and howls and snorts. Bork suddenly released me, and I fell to the ground with a grunt. All my sore bones screamed at me.

"He's *begging* us to eat him!" said a troll.

"We don't really want to eat you. What of you is there to eat?"

"But—" I started.

"Here." Mard, the girl troll, handed me a cup of what looked like steaming mud, or something worse. "You must be hungry, seeing as you were trying to eat those apples. Have some sludge." The sludge was greenish brown and it stank and *moved*. All the trolls were slurping it down like it was honey, but that made it even less appetizing.

I looked down at the sludge and then back up at the trolls. "You're not going to eat me?"

"Eck! Blech!" said a troll, another girl, I thought. It was still hard to tell.

"It's a bit of a joke that humans believe we'll eat them," said Bork.

"And they think they actually *taste* good. So vain."

"But it keeps them away. Mostly."

"Away?"

"Away from us," said Mard. "Humans are trouble dressed up pretty. Especially that greedy idiot King Barf-a-hew or whatever his silly name is."

"What kind of trouble?" I asked. "Humans, I mean 'we,' always thought it was trolls who were trouble."

"And that's the way we like it," said Bork. The other trolls gagged and spit in agreement. "If those greedy humans didn't think we'd gobble them up, they'd try and make slaves out of us."

"Slaves? But why?" I asked. All the trolls looked in different directions and shifted uncomfortably.

"Never mind why," said Mard. "The humans take one look at any living creature and think only of how they can use it."

"So we've made ourselves out to be villains," said Bork. "Isn't that smart?"

"It's not smart if you're going to tell *him*," said a troll wearing a helmet with deer horns. "He's a human too, you know."

"He's not like the rest. Can't you smell it on him?" asked Bork.

"I can," said Deer Horns.

"Smell *what* on me?" I tried to sniff myself. I was pretty dirty, but I couldn't smell anything over the rancid odor of the trolls and their sludge.

The trolls looked at each other cautiously. "Never mind that," said Mard. "We're not going to eat you."

I was still a little suspicious sitting here in the midst of all these trolls who kept saying that I *smelled*. "What were you trying to catch by the apple tree if you don't eat humans?"

"Bork's trying to catch a pet," said Mard. "He's always wanted a pet."

"I wanted a goat," said Bork forlornly. "Not a boy."

"Drink your sludge," said Mard.

I looked down at the cup full of mystery mud. My stomach grumbled, but I wasn't sure I was hungry enough to drink this. I wished I had the meat pie, which was back by the road with Nothing. I thought about those red, juicy apples just sitting on the tree. Maybe trolls didn't like apples. Maybe they thought they tasted like mud and mud tasted like sweet fruit. Maybe they didn't know humans would rather eat apples than mud.

"What's wrong with the apples?" I asked.

"What's wrong with the apples?" said Deer Horns. "Did you ever see an apple tree full of ripe apples this early in the year?"

I thought for a moment. "Actually, I've never seen an apple tree at all. They don't grow on The Mountain, where I'm from. I've only seen apples off the tree."

"Well, that's no ordinary apple tree," said Mard.

Bork leaned over the fire to speak to me. He had as much hair on his arms as I did on my head. "It's *poisoned*," he said. "You could have died . . . or worse. You should thank us."

"Thank you," I said.

"To sludge!" said Bork, lifting his cup. "And no poison apples!" The rest of the trolls grunted, "To sludge!" and they slurped down their drinks. Then they all watched me expectantly. I guess I had to drink it or be considered impolite. What did trolls do with impolite guests? I put it to my mouth and took a sip. It tasted like rotten vegetables, and it was slimy, and I think I swallowed a worm. The trolls all smiled and nodded.

"Ah! That's the stuff!"

"Sets you up for life!"

"Makes you big and strong!"

I wanted to ask more questions, partly because I was curious, but mostly so I wouldn't have to drink more of the sludge. "How do you know the apples are poisoned?" One poisoned apple seemed believable, but an entire *tree* of them was strange.

"Oh, the apples again," said Deer Horns. "We'd best tell him the story, shouldn't we? You tell it, Bork."

"Why me? You tell it, Slop."

"You found the boy," said Deer Horns, or Slop, "and you make the story sound so pretty."

Bork grumbled under his breath, but when he started speaking, his voice was low and dramatic.

"A long time ago, there was a witch, see? She was the queen of some other kingdom far from here—beyond

Yonder—beyond Beyond even! She tried to kill her step-daughter 'cause she was jealous of her beauty."

Gran used to tell me this story, and it was one of my favorites. The girl ran away and lived with dwarves, but the witch-queen found her out and fed her a poisoned apple—one that would make her fall asleep forever. But it didn't work because a prince woke her with true love's first kiss and all that, and she lived happily ever after with her prince. That was where Gran's story ended, but Bork kept going and told a story I didn't know.

"But the witch's poison apple didn't die. The dwarves (careless creatures) threw it down the mountain and it fell in the dirt. Soon that apple was dirt itself, but the *seeds* didn't turn to dirt. Those seeds took root and grew into an apple tree. A magical *poison* apple tree."

"Magic?" I said. "How do you know it's magic?"

The trolls shifted and looked around.

"Because," said Slop as he scratched at his horns, "the fruit is ripe year-round. What but magic could make it ripe all year long?"

They all nodded and grunted in agreement, but I sensed there was something they weren't telling me.

"So if I ate the apples, I would have fallen asleep forever?" I asked.

"Until true love's first kiss, maybe."

That sounded as good as dead to me. True love was for fair princesses and maidens and knights in shining armor. The only girl I was even friends with was Red, and I think she'd rather hit me in the face than kiss me. Maybe she could punch me awake.

"Have you ever seen someone eat those apples?"

"No," said Bork.

"Then how do you know they're poison?" Something about the apples intrigued me.

"A deer ate those apples once," said Slop. "I saw him, and the next day we found him dead." He rubbed the horns on his helmet.

"Wolves got him, Slop," said Bork.

"Those weren't wolves. Those apples ate him from the inside out!"

"Enough about death and fruit!" said Mard. "Eat your sludge." The trolls all got busy slurping and snorting, and so I did my best to blend in by holding my cup to my lips. Every now and then, I spilled a little behind me until my cup was empty.

But unluckily for me, trolls are very hospitable, and Mard took my cup and plunged it into the pot of sludge. She handed it back to me with sludge dripping down the sides. "You need more meat on you. Eat." I ate another worm. It wriggled down my throat.

"So," said another troll as he slurped the last of his sludge. This one looked very old. All the trolls had wrinkles, but this one's skin had wrinkles inside of wrinkles and his tangled hair was streaked with white. "I heard the king got married."

"King Barth-a-hew married?" said Bork. "Who would marry such an ugly thing?"

"I heard the girl can make things gold."

"Straw," I said. "She makes straw into gold."

"A witch," said Slop, the horned troll. "The king married a witch."

"I can smell the trouble from here. I wouldn't get within ten steps of that witch," said Bork.

"Well, people don't come within ten steps of us and we're not bad," said another troll.

"The witch who made that apple was bad," said Bork. Others grunted their agreements.

I wondered if my mother's family in Yonder were all witches. Were they nice witches or mean witches? Maybe Mother was really running from *them*.

"But they're not all bad, are they?" I asked. "Some witches try to help."

"Witches don't help," said Mard. "They just make more trouble."

"*You* would know," said a big troll, and Mard whacked him on the back of the head with her clublike arm. He whacked her back. Then all the trolls started whacking each other, and they rolled and wrestled on the ground. I stood quickly, spilling sludge all down my shirt. A couple of trolls came very near the fire, and sparks flew up in the air before they rolled away laughing in their grunty, snorty way. It seemed this was common troll after-dinner play.

I looked on as the trolls wrestled and snorted and punched each other, almost enjoying the scene, until one troll suddenly sank down into the ground beneath some leaves. All the trolls gasped. Quickly they hauled the troll out and began shoveling leaves over the place where he had fallen. Mard waddled over to me and tried to turn me around, but then another troll slipped on the edge. Soon the entire mass of leaves was scattered, revealing something the trolls did not want me to see. I broke away from Mard.

Beneath the leaves was a hole and in the hole was a huge stash of curious objects: a boot, a mirror, lots of little boxes and trinkets that looked old and valuable, a coil of golden rope that looked oddly like hair, a shimmering cloak, and a golden harp. The harp was playing all by itself.

# CHAPTER TWENTY

## Trolls Smell, but They Also SMELL

The trolls and I stood still and silent for a moment, transfixed by the pile of treasures below. The only sound was the soft tinkling of the harp. "What is all that?" I asked. My words broke the spell.

"Nothing!" they all shouted, and a wall of trolls formed in front of the hole, shuffling me back out of the way.

"The harp is playing by itself," I said, wide-eyed.

"No it isn't. That's the wind."

"The harp is very sensitive to a breeze," said Bork.

All the trolls nodded and grunted their agreement.

"Oh, stop," said Mard. "You might as well explain it to him."

"But . . . our secret," said Bork.

"He *is* the secret," said Mard. "You can smell it all over him."

"Smell *what* on me?" I was getting tired of them

saying I smelled. All I could smell was the rancid reek of trolls.

"Magic," said Mard. "You smell like magic."

"Magic? You can smell . . . magic?" I asked.

"It smells sweet," said Bork, "but also kind of . . . bitter, like a tart berry. It's hard to describe, but the smell is unmistakable and it's all over you."

"Oh," I said, furtively trying to sniff myself to see if I could detect sweetness or bitterness or berries.

"So that means all that stuff in that hole is—"

"Yes," said Bork.

"But you can't have it," said Slop. "You can't even touch it. We're protecting it."

"From what?"

"Humans!" said Mard. "Nasty, meddlesome creatures! They always cause mischief no matter what, but with magic, they cause the most mischief of all. Curses, famines, destruction, madness, and death. One of these days, they're going to turn the whole world into a magical mess."

All the trolls snorted in agreement. "Humans used to make us find it for them," continued Mard. "Slaves, we were—or our ancestors were—kept on chains and sniffing like dogs to find magic things for humans."

"So we started making people believe that we ate humans so they'd leave us alone," said Bork. "My great-great-great-great-great-grandfather Bork is the troll who is hailed for starting it all."

"Says you," said Slop. "For all we know, it was *my* great-great-great-great-great-great-GREAT-grand*mother*."

Bork snorted and continued with his story. "Bork the

Brave he was called. One day as he was sniffing for magic, his master commanded him to eat a magic bean to see what it would do."

"I bet it was poison like those apples," said Slop.

"Don't interrupt," said Bork, and he continued. "Bork wasn't stupid. Trolls may be able to smell the magic, but we don't use it and we certainly don't eat it. Well, I suppose something just snapped in Bork that day. He snatched his own master and said he would eat him instead if the master didn't set him free. Legend has it that he actually did bite him, and the master was so terrified he let Bork go. Soon other trolls learned of Bork's successful escape and they did the same, threatening to eat their masters or their wives and children. One troll even bought his freedom by threatening to eat his master's beloved pet goat.

"Then all sorts of tales were spread about trolls eating their human masters or their wives and children, and soon the trolls were driven from The Kingdom and Yonder and Beyond and anywhere else near humans. Now if we ever come across a human, we pretend we're going to eat them and then we allow them to escape, so they can tell everyone how they were nearly eaten by trolls. It keeps them away, all right."

"But you still look for magic?" I asked.

"Only so we can keep it safe from the humans," said Mard.

"Oh," I said. The trolls were coming closer to me now.

"The smell is strong on you," said Slop. "Even witches don't smell like that. You *reek* of magic."

"Oh," I said again. The trolls all huddled tight around

me, sniffing. Would they throw me into their hoard and guard me too? "Um . . . maybe I should go now? I need to travel to Yonder. To find my family."

"Stay with us tonight," said Mard. "It's too late for travel."

"Yes," said Slop. "And, besides, it's dangerous. You can't be too careful." They pulled me back to their campground like a lost pet.

When it was time to sleep, I learned that the trolls didn't have houses or sleep under any kind of covering. I asked them what they did in the rain and snow. Slop looked at me funny and said, "We let it fall."

Mard piled dry grass on the ground for me and then covered me with giant leaves that had soft fuzz on them, so they were quite cozy. "You'll be safe here," she said.

Exhausted as I was, it was impossible to sleep. The trolls snored like thunder, and their stench only got worse through the night. Troll farts, I discovered, are a hundred times smellier than the human kind.

But it wasn't really the snores or smells that kept me awake. I kept thinking of that pile of magical objects and how the trolls could smell magic. They could smell it on me. And they kept a hoard of magical things hidden away from humans. Could it be that my stiltskin was right here, amongst the trolls?

Silently, I slipped from beneath my bed of leaves and

tiptoed over to the hole. It was covered again. I shoved aside some of the leaves and reached inside. My hand fell on the harp first, but I quickly put that down. If I brought it out, the music might wake the trolls. I didn't see how it could help me anyhow. Of course it was magical, but was it a stiltskin? Did it grow from magic? I touched the boot and brought it out. It was old and worn, with patches and holes. Just a boot. I wondered what would happen if I put it on. I almost stuck my foot inside when I heard a loud grumble and snort. Slop was sitting in a tree right above the hoard.

"A seven-league boot," he said. "Made by a witch in Beyond. Take one step in that and you'll be over the mountains."

"Oh. That would be useful." I could get to Yonder in a blink with this boot, and I could run away if more trouble came along.

"Useful," snorted Slop. "For each step, you'll get a horrible itch that will last for seven years. The last chap who wore that boot has been itching for twenty years. We only got the one boot off of him. He's still wearing the other and still itching."

I held the boot cautiously away from me. Seven years of itching would surely drive a person mad.

"Do all these objects cause bad things?"

"All of them," said Slop. "That mirror, for instance. It will tell you or show you whatever you want."

My heart leapt. I could ask the mirror my name! It could show me where I could find a stiltskin!

"But it will enslave you more and more," said Slop. "Until all you care about is yourself and the mirror. It makes humans twisted and evil."

My heart sank. I did not wish to be twisted and evil. Just whole.

Carefully, I slid the boot back beneath the leaves, and for a moment I thought I caught the smell of the magic, as the trolls had said. It did smell sweet, but also slightly rotten, like spoiled fruit. My mind turned back to the apple tree. Those apples never spoiled. They *grew* from magic. More than anything in this magical hoard, it was the apple tree that sounded like a stiltskin.

I turned to Slop. "So, then, that apple tree, have you ever really seen what its magic does?" I asked.

"Of course," he said. "And it's a terrible magic." He knocked on his helmet.

"Bork said that deer was killed by wolves."

"Well, I never saw wolves. I found the deer dead right by the tree."

"But you didn't actually see the deer eat the apples. Have you ever known a *person* to eat them?"

Slop's face curdled up like sour milk, and he pointed a fat, hairy finger down at me. "Now, listen here, you. I know there's something strange about you. You got a funny smell, different from most humans, but those apples got a funny smell too. Trouble. We trolls know it when we smell it. Those apples aren't meant to be eaten, so you just stay away. Understand?"

I nodded and backed away from Slop and the hoard.

I told him good night and pretended to go back to the camp, but when he was out of sight, I slipped into the darkness of the trees.

I wandered until I found the apple tree. The apples glowed in the darkness, like sparkling jewels growing on the branches. This was absolutely magic—and judging by what the witch had told me, not just any magic. A stiltskin. I could almost smell it, feel it in my bones. But according to the trolls, it was a stiltskin that grew from poison.

I walked around the tree. I took a stick and threw it against the trunk. I reached out and touched one of the branches and then quickly drew back, as though the leaves might burn me. They didn't. Finally, I walked up close and put my hand on the trunk. The tree was so warm I almost thought I could feel it pulsing with life. I swung up and hoisted myself into the branches. Maybe if I stayed here long enough, the magic would rub off on me and make everything better. I waited for a long time, maybe an hour. I felt nothing.

Finally, I reached out and picked an apple. I brought it up to my face. So perfectly smooth. So red. I wondered what Red would say of these apples. She would probably knock the apple from my hand and tell me to leave the magic alone. It would only cause trouble, maybe even death, if the apple was really poison. I didn't want to die. I let the apple fall to the ground, then swung down from the branches and leaned against the trunk. I listened to the deep thrum of the apple tree, which echoed my own heart. Sleep came just as the sky was growing light.

Slop poked me awake with his deer horns. "I sniffed my way right to you," he said. "You must be more trouble than our whole hoard combined."

Slop dragged me back to camp, where the rest of the trolls were waking. They grunted and rubbed their eyes and scratched under their hairy arms.

Mard was stirring a bubbling pot of sludge with one hand, the other hand full of wriggling worms. "You never told us your name. We should know it."

I almost told her my name was Robert, but then I thought if trolls had names like Bork and Slop, Rump couldn't be so bad.

"Rump," I said.

Mard grunted her approval. "Finest human name I've ever heard. They always get so romantic and sentimental," she said, as if she were talking about some other creatures and not my own kind, "giving names as if their children were something fancy to eat: Bartholomew Archibald Reginald Fish Head, or whatever—it's all nonsense. All you need is a sound to distinguish one from the other." She yelled out to two trolls who were just about my size, "Gorp! Grot! Out of the stream and into the mud!"

"But what about destiny?" I asked.

Mard snorted. "Less is always more." She threw the worms into the pot and then scooped up a cup and handed it to me. I stared at my moving drink.

"Do you ever eat anything else?" I asked.

"Sludge is good for you. Simple to cook and it makes

you strong and wise. Humans, they make everything complicated. Even food."

"Doesn't life ever get complicated for trolls?"

Mard shook her head. "When trolls were enslaved by humans, maybe. But we don't worry about a lot of the things humans fuss over. Simple needs make a simple life."

Simple. They couldn't possibly understand how complicated things already were for me, both inside and out. It's hard to make simple out of complicated, like trying to make a straight line out of a tangled knot. You don't even know where to start.

I drank sludge with the trolls (it wasn't so bad the second time), and then Slop threw a mud ball and it splattered all over Bork's face. Bork threw mud back, and then the rest joined in and mud was flying everywhere. I thought that might be a good time for me to get on my way, but I got pelted with a mud ball and I couldn't just stand there, so I hurled one back, and then Gorp and Grot threw me into a mud puddle. I laughed as they rolled me in the mud, and I saw now why they bathed in it. The mud smelled better than they did.

Now that I was certain the trolls wouldn't eat him, I brought Nothing into the camp (he was still on the road eating grass). The trolls snorted with delight, especially Bork, who took to him right away. Amazingly, Nothing did what Bork wanted! He walked without being pulled. Bork rode on him and Nothing moved!

"He likes my sounds," said Bork. "It makes him feel that we are equals."

I guessed I would have to start snorting and grunting

if I wanted to get anywhere with Nothing, but then I had a better idea.

"You can keep him," I said. "I know he's not a goat, but he'll be happy here, and I can travel faster without him."

Bork rubbed Nothing on the neck and smiled, showing yellow pointy teeth. "It is a big trade for a cup of sludge."

"Well . . . and saving me from eating poison apples."

Bork grunted and I took that as a yes. I untied my satchel from Nothing, then patted his rump and told him goodbye. He hee-hawed and I guessed he was saying, "Good riddance!"

I made my goodbyes. Some of the trolls tried to convince me to stay one more night, but I didn't think I could eat any more sludge, and I was so tired I couldn't put up with their snores and smells for another night.

"Take some sludge for your journey," said Mard, handing me a small jug. "Maybe it will help make things a little simpler for you."

"Oh . . . thank you." I swallowed a gag. "Thank you for not eating me." They all grunted and snorted, and even though I knew they were laughing, it still sounded horrible.

With my satchel slung over one arm and the sludge in my other hand, I headed down the road toward Yonder. I felt a little envious of the trolls and their simple life. My destiny didn't allow for simple. What was behind me and what was ahead of me felt like nothing but snarled knots of complicated.

# CHAPTER TWENTY-ONE

## Yonder

Dear Rump,
    The miller has been lorded now. I refuse to call
him Lord Oswald. He will always be the fat, greedy
miller, and his sons are still ugly trolls.
                                    Your friend,
                                    Red

I had to laugh. If Red could meet real trolls, she'd see
that they were much nicer than Frederick and
Bruno—and less ugly besides.

The gnome found me after dark when I stopped by
the side of the road to rest. I sent a return message explaining where I was going. I told Red if she contacted
me again (which of course she didn't have to as it might

not get to me, anyway), *not* to tell me anything about Opal and babies. *Ever.*

After a hard day's travel and nothing to eat but sludge, I thought I definitely deserved to eat Martha's meat pie. It was only slightly stale, and I slept better than I had in ages.

The next day I found a stream not far from the road, but nothing to eat, so I drank some of Mard's sludge. It wriggled all the way down, but it was food.

For three days I traveled and didn't meet a soul, but on the fourth morning the road split in two directions. One sign pointed to "Yonder" and another pointed to "Beyond." My heart skipped a few beats. Yonder! It seemed as good as finding a mother or a stiltskin—and maybe Yonder had them both!

By afternoon I started to hear the bleating of goats and the mooing of cows. But before long the baaing of sheep drowned them all out. Sheep were everywhere, grazing in green fields, lazing beneath trees, or drinking at the stream.

My stomach grumbled. I hadn't eaten since I finished off the trolls' sludge yesterday morning. I wondered if I could slip into the pasture and milk one of the cows. Probably not without getting kicked.

I walked through a small village where chickens and gnomes were scattered among little houses with thatched roofs and smoking chimneys. Women were hanging laundry out to dry while children danced around, chasing pixies.

I approached an older woman shaking out a rug. I

told her I was looking for someone who might know my mother. "She's dead, but she lived in Yonder and I want to find her family."

The woman took stock of my tattered clothes and overall filthiness. She recoiled slightly. I must have smelled like trolls. "What was her name?" the woman asked.

"Anna," I said.

"I don't know her," she said. "But there's another village about five miles yonder that has a fair amount of merchants and peddlers. When you come to a fork in the road, take the left."

"Thank you," I said, and started to leave, but then my stomach reminded me to ask, "Do you have any food you could spare? I've been traveling a long time."

The woman hesitated but then nodded. "Wait a moment." When she came back, she handed me a slice of bread and a slab of goat's cheese.

I wished there was something I could offer in return. But all I had was Opal's jewels, which might raise the woman's suspicion and would definitely require far too much explanation—or a load of lies. So I simply gave her my thanks, and went on my way.

As soon as I was out of the woman's sight, I walked down by the stream and shoved the bread and cheese in my mouth. The way I looked, I doubted anyone would be very helpful, so I washed as much dirt and grime and troll smell off me as I could. But the downside of being clean was that the pixies instantly flew to me, and I had to walk with them fluttering all over my head and around my body. Their shrill voices rang in my ears.

I reached the other village in late afternoon. It reminded me of my village on The Mountain. Little lopsided houses were scattered willy-nilly, and the only big building was the mill, which stood on the edge of a forest. People were outside milking cows and shearing sheep, and planting seeds in their gardens. They were lucky they could grow their own food.

I stopped a man on the street and asked him if he knew of a woman who lived there years ago named Anna. He said no. I asked more people and they all said no. Finally in frustration I slumped against a rickety fence. All my hope was slowly seeping out of me. I brushed some pixies from my face and arms. But they just came back, giggling.

"You must be full of luck," said a voice behind me.

I turned and stared through the fence. There was an old man sitting in front of a wooden shack, spinning. Seeing someone spinning renewed my hope. Maybe I shouldn't ask just about my mother, but about the kind of work she did.

"Luck?" I asked the man, brushing a pixie from my nose.

"The pixies, they bring luck," said the man.

I snorted. "I'm the most unlucky person I know."

"Luck can change."

I watched him spin, rhythmically twisting the wool. "Are there many here who spin?"

"A fair few. We have a lot of wool."

Yes, of course. All those sheep. I opened the gate and stepped closer to the man and his spinning wheel. Just ordinary wool.

"And do they all spin the same way as you?"

"Well, I suppose a few have lost a finger or two in the business, but mostly we all get on the same. Not much to it."

"But I've heard tales . . . stories of those who can spin wonderful things. Not regular yarn, but more . . . uh . . . valuable things."

The man stopped his spinning and looked up at me with pale, penetrating eyes.

I stepped back.

"You're speakin' of the Wool Witches?"

"The Wool Witches? Is there such a thing?"

"Oh yes," he said with a laugh. "And they're witches, all right, can turn wool into silk and grass into silver! Their work is quite fine, though I've never seen it. They travel to trade it. Won't trade with anyone they know. They live there, in those woods." He pointed in the direction of the mill.

Witches must like to live hidden in trees.

"Thank you," I said, and turned to leave.

"Watch your step," said the old man.

I froze. "Excuse me?"

"You're stepping in my wool," he said, pointing to my feet.

"Oh . . . right. Sorry. . . . Thank you."

I walked through the little village and kept my eyes on the ground. I could feel the stares on the back of my head.

I guessed they didn't get many visitors. Well, we never did on The Mountain, either. I glanced up as I passed the mill. A girl sat outside combing through wool. She reminded me of Opal. Opal and bargains and babies. My stomach twisted. I looked back down at the ground and stepped into the trees.

There was a dusty little road leading into the woods, but soon it became a narrow, rocky trail, which twisted and wound until I thought I might be going in circles. Then the trail faded altogether, and I wondered if it was one of those tricky paths Red used to find her granny. These were witches, after all.

Pixies flitted about my nose and buzzed in my ears. Maybe I should roll in the mud again. Maybe I should find the path and go back, but then I saw smoke rising in the distance. As I drew closer, the pixies seemed to multiply, and they danced and squealed all around me. Finally, I came to a little cottage with flowers blossoming along the hedge and a stone path that led to a door painted bright red.

A red door was a bad sign. I felt all hot and twitchy. I shouldn't be here. These witches might not know anything about my mother. They might not know anything about my kind of spinning. And they might not be nice.

Before I could change my mind, the door flew open and a girl stepped outside. She squealed in delight. "A visitor! Oh, do come in! We have cake!"

# CHAPTER TWENTY-TWO

## The Wool Witches

The girl grabbed me by the arm and yanked me inside. The first thing I noticed was a delicious smell, sweet and spicy. My stomach growled. Food. Real food.

The room was large, but it was many rooms in one, just like my cottage: the kitchen, the bedroom, and the sitting room all occupied their own corners of one big open room, which was bursting with colors and patterns. Sunlight poured in from three tall windows, their curtains intricately embroidered with vines, birds, and blossoms. Four chairs circled a big oak table. They were painted in bright blue, violet, yellow, and green, and each was built in its own unique style and shape, as if they had been designed for very different people. A large bed took up an entire wall and was covered with a blanket woven in rich rainbow colors. The room seemed to hum as if it were alive.

"Now, what is your name?" the girl asked. "No, let me guess! I love guessing names." She put her fingers to her mouth and studied me. She was maybe just a few years older than me, and pretty, with black curls all around her face and eyes as green as new spring grass. "Your name is . . . Herbert. No, no, you don't look like a Herbert. Bertram? No, you don't have the right aura for that. Ooh, tricky, tricky! Something unusual—one of a kind, I think. Zelgemeier? Woldenecht? Rolfando?"

"Ida, who is it?" said a voice coming through a small doorway to the right. Another woman entered who looked very much like the girl, but older. She had gray streaked in her black hair and lines around her mouth and eyes. When she saw me, she froze. "Oh my."

The woman closed her eyes and took a deep breath and then opened them again.

"What is it, Sister?" said Ida.

"Hadel! Come here!" the older woman shouted.

Another woman came hobbling in. This one looked more like a witch to me. She wasn't so old, but she was hunched and she had a cane and one foot was turned in. Her face was lopsided: one eye squinting while the other was wide. Her mouth was pinched and cross, but when her big eye was level with mine, her expression softened and her mouth hung open.

"Do you see it?" said the second woman.

"See what?" said Ida.

"Anna," said the lopsided witch.

"Anna was my mother," I explained.

Ida gasped. It was as if they had all been frozen by some spell. Shocked into silence. I felt like an idiot.

Finally, Ida broke into a laugh. "Nephew!" She rushed to me and crushed me against her, which might have felt comforting if I could breathe. When she released me, she squeezed my cheeks between her hands and said, "Isn't he beautiful? Our nephew, Sisters! Anna's son! Who could ever have known?"

The second sister blinked and came to me. She reached out a finger and lifted my chin.

"He looks very much like Anna, doesn't he, Hadel?"

Hadel finally broke from her stupor as well, but she didn't come to me. She paused, looking me over with her big eye, and then grumbled, "I don't see it as something to rejoice over." She hobbled out of the room. Ida's cheerful face fell, and her older sister looked at me with a suspicious frown. This was a mistake. They didn't want me here. I shouldn't have come. I took a step back, but Ida caught me by the shoulder.

"Oh, don't mind Hadel, dear nephew," said Ida. "She has always been crabby. This is Balthilda. We are so glad you came to us! You may call me Aunty Ida. Come and have ca—"

"Ida, we know nothing of the boy," Balthilda cut in, "where he came from, how he found us, or even what his name is."

"His name." Ida's face darkened. "I've been unable to guess it. So curious. I'm usually spot-on."

I looked between them. I was so tired, the idea of

trying to explain my name and everything else over-whelmed me. I didn't really want to see the look on their faces. "My name is Robert."

Balthilda furrowed her brow, confused.

"Well," said Ida, looking disappointed, "I never would have guessed that."

"How is it that you found us, Robert?" asked Balthilda.

"I asked in the village about my mother. Nobody re-membered her, but when I asked about spinning . . ."

Balthilda stiffened, but nodded. They must know about my mother's spinning.

"Oh, but come eat cake and see what we are making!" Ida dragged me through a small corridor leading to an-other room, but Hadel barred the doorway with her walk-ing stick. "You're filthy!" she growled.

"Hadel, Robert is our nephew and our guest!"

Hadel's big eyes looked me up and down, and I felt that she could see every secret I held. "Hmph. Robert, you'll take a bath before you set foot in here. You look like you grew from dirt!"

The bathtub was in a corner of the kitchen. Balthilda poured hot water in the tub and held out soap and a brush to scrub myself. Then she and Ida left the room through the doorway where Hadel had gone.

After I washed, my clothes were hanging to dry by the fire, so I wrapped myself in a quilt sewn with a hundred different colors.

"I made that," said Ida when she returned. "Do you like it?"

"How do you get so many colors?" I asked, brushing my hands over the intricate patterns.

"It's all in the fingertips. Wait until you see what I'm working on now."

While my clothes dried, Ida fed me as much food as I could shove into my mouth, which was a lot. Not only had I forgotten what it was like to be clean, I had forgotten what it was like to eat real food instead of wormy sludge. And this food was even better than the food I remembered eating—better than Martha's meat pies, or Red's granny's stew. It was certainly better than sludge. There were beets and potatoes sprinkled with herbs and cheese, fresh bread, and milk. I'd never had cake before, but it turned out to be a sort of bread that was sweet and crumbly and moist. I had three helpings.

I was feeling rather sleepy after I ate, especially when I put on my warm, freshly cleaned clothes, but Ida had other ideas. She pulled me into the other room, where Hadel and Balthilda were. I stopped in the doorway and gaped.

Hadel sat at a spinning wheel, and piled at her feet were skeins of threads in colors that no dye could make. Red brighter than strawberries, yellow like sunshine, blue like the morning sky and blue like deep water, green like the forest leaves, and all shades in between, colors I had never seen in the world.

Balthilda was knitting what looked like a shawl, creating a fluid and intricate pattern with Hadel's rich threads. She worked with such speed and rhythm, her fingers and knitting needles became a blur.

But what amazed me the most were the tapestries. Every inch of the walls was covered with bright pictures full of life: a white unicorn in a field of orange poppies, dancing princesses, a knight shielding the red fire of a dragon, a maiden in a tower. In the middle of the room was a big loom, strung with varying shades of threads. Ida went and sat behind the loom, moving her hands across the strings, weaving her threads in and out and around each other. As she drew the fibers together, they created vibrant pictures—birds and pixies and flowers—and they were so lifelike they seemed to breathe and move as if in a gentle breeze. Surely, this was magic. Magic like how I spun the gold, and how my mother had.

As I watched, I had a tingling sensation in my toes and fingers, my head and my chest. This was where everything started, where I started. It all began with my mother, and she began here.

"How does it work?" I asked.

"Enchantments," Ida said with a thrill in her voice. "Magic."

"Ida," said Balthilda. It sounded like a warning.

"We do more of our own work than the magic does," said Ida. "We just allow enough enchantment to give the fibers a nudge."

"You're nudging a little hard there, don't you think?" said Hadel. She had been spinning wool into a gentle shade of lavender, but as she spoke, the color deepened to a violent purple.

"It will fetch a good price at the market," said Ida.

"Yes, but at what cost to you?"

"Oh, Hadel, you worry too much. There is no greed or pride in this, only beauty."

Hadel glared at the tapestry but continued with her spinning, and as she fell back into the rhythm, her threads lightened back to lavender.

"Can you only change the color of the threads?" I asked. "Or can you change what they're made of?"

"A little, but not too much," said Hadel. "I would never be so foolish or greedy." She eyed me, and again, I felt that she could see right down inside me, to the foolishness and greed that had gotten me into so much trouble.

"Hadel is very cautious," said Ida.

"We would all do well to be cautious, considering what happened to his mother," Hadel said, nodding toward me.

Balthilda put her knitting down. "Hadel. It could happen to anyone."

"Anyone foolish enough to be so greedy."

"Anyone can be greedy," said Ida.

"Clearly," said Hadel.

"Excuse me," I said, "but I never knew my mother—"

"Oh! You poor thing! We are being insensitive," said Ida. She dropped her work and rushed to comfort me.

"No, it isn't that. It's just . . . Well, I hardly know anything about her. I knew that she was from Yonder and that she could spin. Her spinning wasn't like other people's, but how was she foolish and greedy?" The three aunts stopped what they were doing and exchanged cautious looks.

"Did she make any of this?" I asked, pointing to the tapestries and yarns.

"No," said Balthilda. "She traded everything she made."

"Including her soul," mumbled Hadel under her breath.

"Hadel!" gasped Ida. "Our poor nephew!"

"Well, he's poor because of her. Don't you think he has a right to know?"

They all fell silent. Balthilda and Ida stared at the ground, but Hadel watched me, her big eye twitching.

"I know about her spinning," I spoke up again, dancing around the questions I most wanted to ask. I wanted to know what had happened to my mother. I wanted to know if there was anything that could be done about my problems, but I couldn't decide how much I wanted *them* to know about *me*. "I know that she could spin . . . valuable things. Will you tell me what happened to her?"

"Greed," said Hadel. "Greed and magic sucked her in and spun her to death."

"Hadel, be sensitive," said Ida.

"It's the truth. You were too young to understand."

Ida opened her mouth in protest, but Balthilda cut her off. "She was a fine spinner," said Balthilda in a gentle voice, "the finest there has ever been in Yonder or anywhere."

"Not so fine, considering," said Hadel.

Balthilda glared at Hadel and began again. "I will say she was unwise, and a bit overly confident, even though she was a fine spinner, and that is where the trouble began. You see, Robert, in our work we must balance the skill of our own hands with the magic we use to transform the threads." She held out her knitting as if to show me. "We do not call for more magic than we have skill, because then we lose control of the outcome. We lose control of ourselves." I thought of poor Kessler, and the sick dread in my stomach returned. "Anna knew this, but she always pushed the limits. She was always experimenting."

"How?" I asked.

Balthilda put down her knitting and swept a strand of graying hair back from her face. "Your mother could spin wool into velvet and grass into silk. Beautiful threads. Her work was much admired, but we feared she was losing the balance. Yet somehow it never seemed to affect her. She always managed to bargain well at the markets, so in spite of our warning, Anna came to believe that her skill was more powerful than any magic."

"She thought she could control it, you mean?"

Balthilda nodded. "One day Anna told a wealthy merchant that she could spin any worthless thing into something beautiful and valuable. Well, he took her at her word. He had a bundle of straw in his cart and said he would be pleased with her skill only if she could turn the straw into gold. He promised her a fair trade if she could fulfill the task."

"I warned her, that fool," said Hadel, "but she was all pride and greed."

"It was dangerous, to be sure," continued Balthilda.

"But she couldn't have known just how dangerous," said Ida. "It wasn't her fault. That merchant was the greedy one!"

"When she told me of the bargain she had made, I truly hoped she would fail," said Balthilda. "Velvet and linen and silk were one thing, but gold? I didn't think it possible. I hoped it wasn't, but to my dismay, Anna succeeded beyond what I ever could have imagined. She spun that straw into gold, into perfect glimmering skeins of gold more pure than any gold in The Kingdom. But even her skill could not match the enormous magic of spinning straw into gold."

All three sisters looked down, filled with an unspoken grief.

"Was the merchant's trade fair?" I asked.

Hadel blew through her lips like a horse. "Fair! That man swindled her to pieces! When he came and demanded what had been made of his straw, of course he was delighted, and what's more, Anna had no power to demand a fair bargain. *That's* what happens when you get greedy with the magic. You lose control. The merchant gave her a sack of grain for her pile of gold, declaring that it was a fair trade, for without *his* straw she would've had nothing to spin."

I shivered, remembering the first time I had traded with the miller, how my tongue had swelled in my mouth and I mechanically accepted his bargain. I didn't understand then what it all meant.

"I remember that day," said Ida. "I was small, but I remember her nearly fainting as she held that sack of grain. Her face! She looked as though she had seen death."

"You'd think she would have stopped there," said Hadel. "But, no, she was determined to be the greediest wench there ever was."

"Hadel, you mustn't speak so of our sister. She only thought to remedy her mistake," said Ida.

"Yes, well, it didn't work, did it?"

I felt as if all my past troubles were being laid out before me, troubles I well knew, and I was waiting, hoping for them to tell me the solution. "What happened?"

Balthilda's eyes glistened with tears. She fumbled with her knitting and brought it close to her face, as if her work would keep her emotions at bay.

"She didn't believe she had lost control because of the magic. She claimed it was because the merchant had given her the straw. She spun more gold, this time from her own straw, thinking she could negotiate the terms of the trade, but she couldn't. She took that gold thread to the markets and sold it for a pittance. People always start a bargain ridiculously low, and Anna had no power to refuse or suggest a price. Whatever they offered, she had to take, and the gold was theirs."

I knew that feeling. I was blind to it at first, but with Opal, I recalled the powerlessness I felt at not being able to suggest a trade, or even refuse one I thought abominable.

"Then the merchant returned," growled Hadel.

"Yes. That was truly the worst part," said Balthilda.

"He returned with a wagon full of straw for Anna to spin," said Ida. "I remember that. So much straw, and I knew what he wanted. I knew!"

This merchant was sounding a lot like the miller.

"Anna refused," said Balthilda. "But the merchant

told her he was on his way to The Kingdom and he was certain that King Herbertus, the ruler at the time, would be interested to know of Anna's great skill. It was a threat she couldn't live with. Anna was so fiercely independent, and she knew that any king would want to use her skill for his own gain. So she spun the gold for the merchant once more, and for payment, he gave her a new spinning wheel, so that she might spin for him on many more occasions."

"Rumpel," said Hadel. "She was locked in a rumpel then."

Her voice was so soft I almost didn't hear her. "What? She was locked in what?"

"*Rumpel.* That's what we call our own work sometimes. It means wrapped or trapped in magic. We wrap our work in magic; only your mother did it to herself: she spun herself in magic so tight it killed her."

"Oh, Hadel, that's ridiculous!" said Ida. "A *person* can't be trapped in a rumpel! And I'm sure Anna didn't spin again once she left. She probably died in childbirth."

"She died right after I was born," I said.

"See?"

"You think that, Ida, if it gives you comfort. But I say once you've become unbalanced in the magic, rumpel grabs you and spins you fast and tight, so that it's impossible to get out. It suffocates you. She was never free of it, no matter what she died from. A rumpel never lets go." Hadel fixed her crooked gaze on me until a chill ran up my neck and through my bones.

"What happened then?" I asked.

"She knew the merchant would never leave her alone,"

said Balthilda. "So she ran away that very afternoon. She told no one where she was going, and she took nothing with her but the wheel from the merchant."

"I begged her not to go," said Ida as she wiped tears from her eyes. "I ran down the road, crying for her. I waited outside for days for her to return. Ooh, I'd like to wrap my threads around that merchant's fat, greedy neck!" She twisted the threads in her hands.

"The last we heard was that she had married a man from far away and she died shortly after of illness. We never knew she had a son. . . ."

They kept talking, but their words faded from me. Rumpel. Was that what my mother had named me? Because she was trapped in the magic, and she knew I would be too. It made sense to me, but it didn't bring me any comfort. I didn't feel like more of a person, smarter or bigger like I always hoped I would. I felt smaller and more alone than ever.

"Come, Robert, you must be exhausted." Ida pulled me to my feet and led me back to the kitchen. "Here we are, nice and cozy." In a corner near the hearth, there was a little bed made of a pile of straw and two blankets woven with blue-and-green wool. I stared at the straw and shivered.

Ida frowned and bit her lip. "My sisters and I share a bed. I'm sorry we don't have another. I thought you would be most comfortable here."

"Oh," I said, forcing a smile. I didn't want to seem ungrateful. "It's wonderful, really. Straw is so . . . warm."

Ida stared at me for a moment. She had been so kind

and excited when I came, but now I could see the wariness in her eyes too. "Good night, Robert." She left me with only the last glows of the coals for light.

Every part of me was exhausted as I slumped down in the straw bed and closed my eyes. I was too tired to think. The only thing I had in my mind as I drifted off to sleep was the drumming of a single word, over and over. *Rumpel, Rumpel, Rumpel . . .*

# CHAPTER TWENTY-THREE

## Growing Crazy

I woke to hushed voices in the dark. Where was I? Who was there? Was I in danger? My heart pounded and then I remembered. I was with the Wool Witches, my aunts, my mother's sisters. They had just told me how she died and why I was the way I was. They had told me my name.

Rumpel.

My aunts' whispers carried from the opposite corner of the room. I couldn't see them, but I strained to hear their voices.

"He's not telling us something," whispered Hadel.

"What would you have him tell us? Anna died when he was just a baby. He knew nothing of her troubles."

"Anna died, but that doesn't mean her trouble died with her. If she was in a rumpel—"

"Oh, stop! She was not trapped in a rumpel!"

"You don't understand," said Hadel. "If she was in a

rumpel when the boy was born, the magic wouldn't have died with her. It would affect her child too."

"You think the boy is in a rumpel too?" Balthilda asked.

"Oh, don't be ridiculous!" hissed Ida. "He probably has a gift just as Anna did. We could teach him our work, only this time—"

"No!" said Hadel in a harsh whisper. "That would only bring trouble for all of us. And, besides, who knows what *he* is running from?"

Silence passed for a minute, and then Ida spoke. "Do you think he came to us for help?"

Hadel spoke gravely. "A rumpel is deep magic. If it has been the boy's state since birth, it would be all the stronger."

"The knowledge must have tortured Anna," said Balthilda. "Oh, how she must have suffered!"

"She deserved it," said Hadel.

"Shame, Hadel!" snapped Ida. "No one deserves such suffering. No one!"

"Perhaps we should question him," said Balthilda.

"He would tell us if he wanted us to know," said Ida. "Let him be."

"Don't we have a right to know? If he's running from something, it will catch up to him. You can't hide from a rumpel."

"But he's so small and young," said Ida. "We must be able to help him."

"We couldn't help Anna," said Balthilda. "There was nothing for us to do."

"Who knows what the boy will do to us," said Hadel.

They all fell silent then and didn't speak anymore. Soon I heard the rhythm of their snores, but I stayed awake for a long time, thinking over their words, thinking on one word. A name. *Rumpel.* I was certain now. Rumpel was my name, because that's what I was. This was why I could spin the gold. This was why the trolls could smell so much magic on me. I was born in the magic, trapped inside of it. What had been my mother's purpose in giving me such a name? Was it a warning? A cry of despair? Or maybe just the cold, hard truth.

Balthilda said there was no help for a rumpel. Had The Witch of The Woods known about rumpels? Did my aunts know about stiltskins? If I found one, could it still set me free? And would my aunts even allow me to stay? I might bring danger to them, as they said, but I had nowhere to go. These were my mother's sisters. They were the only family I had in the world.

I wrapped the blankets tighter around me, trying to feel warm and safe, but I only felt alone, shivering with fear. I wished more than anything that I were back on The Mountain with Gran sitting by the fireplace telling me stories about other people's magic troubles.

My aunts were talking again when I woke the next morning. They sat around the table in their chairs: Hadel in the blue, Balthilda in the violet, and Ida in the yellow. That must mean the green chair had been my mother's.

When my aunts saw me, they grew quiet. Hadel very deliberately inspected my pile of hay, as if I might have turned it to gold just by sleeping in it.

Ida handed me two slices of bread for breakfast. "Did you sleep well?" she asked with a searching look, as if she were trying to see the rumpel that bound me.

"Yes, thank you," I said, taking the bread and sitting down in the green chair. No one spoke another word for the rest of breakfast.

My aunts busied themselves with their work—baking bread, combing wool, and sweeping the dirt out the door. When I offered to help with the chores, Ida warmed considerably, and she was delighted when I said I could milk a goat. She handed me a bucket. "Eloise is grazing in the back."

"Eloise?"

"The goat, of course. Her name is Eloise."

"I never heard of an animal with a name." Calling our goat Milk and our donkey Nothing was strange enough, but giving an animal a name you would give a human was unheard of.

"Haven't you?" asked Ida. "How silly. How can we expect them to give us any respect or work if we don't give them a proper name? Common sense."

I thought she was crazy until I milked Eloise. She filled the bucket to the brim. Milk couldn't have filled an inch. Maybe Nothing would have been a little less ornery if I'd given him a proper name. He probably didn't like being called Nothing any more than I liked being called Rump.

That night I sat with my aunts again as they worked.

Ida was weaving the same tapestry from the night before, and as she formed pixies with her threads, I could almost hear their squeals and giggles. Balthilda was knitting something different tonight, something with green fabric, though I couldn't tell what it was. Hadel sat in a dim corner spinning, but her wool glowed as it wrapped on the bobbin so it shone through the darkness.

My fingertips tingled as I watched, like they itched to spin. I curled my fingers into tight fists, trying to crush that feeling out of me. Hadel looked up, her big eye boring into me. I turned back to Ida.

"Can you tell me more about how it works?" I asked Ida.

Ida smiled, full of delight, like she'd been waiting her whole life to show someone and explain what she could do. "Think of drawing water from a well. You pull the magic inside of you as one might pull the water up from the well, slow and steady. You try to measure what you can do on your own, and then you imagine what you would like the magic to improve. Then you pour the magic from your fingers right into the threads—not too much, though, just a little spark." Her hands moved quickly over the loom, pulling threads in and out, the colors swirling and shimmering.

"Where do you pull the magic from?"

"Everywhere!" She laughed. "Magic is everywhere. In the air, in the ground, in fire and water and the stars and clouds and the sun. The sun is bursting with magic. You pull it in from all around you."

"How?"

"Like you pull air into your lungs."

"What if you pull too much in?"

"Well, I . . ." Ida hesitated. "You push it back. You can feel when it starts to overwhelm you."

"But how do you push it back?"

She looked confused. I could tell she was trying to explain something she had always known how to do, but didn't know exactly how she did it. Like seeing or smelling or wiggling your fingers.

"You just push it back."

"And what happens if you don't push it back? What if you let it overwhelm you?"

"Then you get into trouble," said Hadel in a gruff voice. "Like your mother."

I didn't ask any more questions.

I studied my aunts' work very intently for the next few nights. Mostly, I wanted to watch Hadel, to see her pull the magic in and push it back as she spun. But she was difficult to watch because that big eye of hers always caught me with a cold stare that made me shiver. So I watched Ida and Balthilda work instead. I focused on their fingers, trying to see how the magic came in, but I saw nothing. Although there were no sparks or flames, it all looked like magic to me.

I tried to forget about spinning gold, and the next week Ida and Balthilda helped take my mind off things by surprising me with new clothes—two sets of them! Who besides nobles and kings and princesses owned two sets of clothes? Ida wove the fabric on her loom and then cut and sewed it: brown and blue woolen pants and two shirts. Balthilda presented me with two knitted sweaters, one with many colors interwoven, and one green, bright but somehow calm, like spring on The Mountain. The green was my favorite.

"Hadel spun that green just for you," said Ida.

"Thank you," I said.

Hadel grunted, "It's the color of your eyes."

"You have your mother's eyes," said Balthilda.

"So we hope it's a good *surprise*," said Ida, emphasizing the rhyme, which made me smile. I guess rhymes must run in the family.

As I folded up the sweater, I wondered what my mother had been like. How she smiled and laughed. Did she make up rhymes too? My aunts rarely mentioned her, and when they did, it was always with sadness or, in Hadel's case, anger. I imagined that my mother had looked a lot like Ida with her black hair and merry smile.

"Do I look anything like Mother?" I asked her. "Besides my eyes, that is."

Ida shook her head. "The rest of you must look like your father. I'll wager he was handsome."

"I never knew him, either. He died before I was born, in the mines."

"Then who has been caring for you all these years?"

"My gran, but she's gone now too."

Ida's eyes swam with tears. "Oh! You poor thing! Nothing sad should ever happen to you again." And she squeezed me so tight I started seeing sparks. I liked Ida, but I wasn't sure I liked all the crying and squeezing girls seemed so fond of. I missed Red.

After a few weeks, my aunts became less wary of me and we settled into a routine. Ida was the sweetest toward me, and she made sure to put huge amounts of food in front of me, which I ate and ate. Balthilda was kind but quiet, and Hadel stayed as far away from me as possible. If I ever came near, her big eye got bigger and her squinty eye crinkled up like a knot on a tree. She seemed to think I was contagious. And I never forgot her words: *You can't hide from a rumpel.*

The spring turned to summer, and instead of spinning and weaving and knitting by fires, my aunts did their work by open windows, waiting for a breeze to come in. The problem with open windows was the pixies.

"Oh, these pixies!" said Ida, brushing a green-haired, fuzzy-winged pixie off her loom. "I do think they are worse this year."

"Yes," said Hadel, and she eyed me as several pixies rested on my shirt.

"Why do pixies like it so much here?" I asked innocently.

"They like the bright colors," said Balthilda. "Color and shine are the next best thing to gold for a pixie, so we usually have more than our fair share"—she swatted one away—"but they've never been quite this bad."

I now had three pixies fluttering around my head. Ever so faintly, I heard one of them chanting for gold in its tiny voice. I hoped my aunts didn't notice.

It became my job to shoo the pixies outside. I waited by the window with a rag, flicking it at them every time they came near. They usually laughed and it became a game, but sometimes I'd give a pixie a good *whack* and it would flip through the air and fly away topsy-turvy. I kind of enjoyed it.

On cool days, when the windows were shut, I would help my aunts with their work. Balthilda had me hold her yarns so they wouldn't tangle as she knit, and sometimes I would arrange Hadel's yarns according to their shades.

Helping Ida was my favorite. She'd let me pick colors for her loom or suggest a picture she could put into a tapestry. I suggested trolls once, but she didn't like that idea, so I asked her to make an apple tree. When she finished, it looked so real I almost thought I could reach into the tapestry, pluck an apple, and take a bite. It looked just like the magical apple tree in the trolls' forest.

Ida and I made rhymes as we worked. She was clever with her words, and we tossed the rhymes back and forth. This one was my favorite:

> *In Yonder there lived three lovely witches*
> *Who spun and wove and sewed little stitches*
> *Together they made me a new pair of britches*
> *Just the right size with no snags to cause itches*
> *But don't let the witches*
> *Make straw into riches*
> *Because witches' riches*
> *Cause glitches*

Ida and I got so used to speaking in rhyme, sometimes we didn't even realize we were doing it.

"There's a pixie on your head."

"He must see a thread."

"I'll swat him away."

"Please, don't delay!"

One morning, when I tried to pull my pants up, they rose above my ankles.

"My pants have shrunk!" I cried to my aunts. I danced around in them. They were tight and uncomfortable.

Aunt Ida laughed and then cupped her hands over her mouth.

"Nothing happened to your pants," said Hadel. "You did that yourself."

"I didn't shrink my pants."

Ida shook her head and laughed. "Robert, look at yourself. You grew!"

I stopped hopping and almost fell over. "I . . . what?"

"For all you eat, how can you be surprised?" said Hadel. "A cow can't eat as much as you."

I stared down at my feet with the pants hanging a few inches above my ankles, then glanced over at Ida. When I had first come, I barely reached her chest. Now my nose was level with her shoulder.

"But I don't grow," I said in disbelief.

"You do now," laughed Ida. "Eat your oatmeal before it gets cold!"

I was excited—and confused. I had grown! Was it because I knew the rest of my name? That must be it.

I was so happy at the thought, I almost forgot about

everything else—the spinning, the gold, the rumpel, and Opal's promise to me. Somehow the growth made me think other things had changed too. Maybe I wasn't as trapped anymore.

That morning I ate two bowls of oatmeal, filling my belly to bursting. I could almost feel myself growing! I was halfway through a third bowl when Ida spilled her gossip from the markets.

"The new queen is with child," she said excitedly.

I choked on my oatmeal, coughed, and spit it out.

"Hope he's not as big an oaf as his father," grumbled Hadel.

"Who says it will be a boy?" asked Ida. "Perhaps we shall have a little princess."

My stomach clenched, and I pushed away my oatmeal. My aunts' conversation faded from my ears as a strange feeling came over me. Inside me I felt little threads, growing and spreading and knotting together, tangling me up and binding me tight. It was the rumpel—my curse.

The threads stayed tangled tight inside me all day.

My only hope was to keep myself hidden so I wouldn't find out when the baby was born. If I never heard of the baby being born, I might not need to take it. My aunts were far from The Kingdom. They didn't get little news, but they got big news, and a royal baby was big news. There was no way that I could avoid hearing of the baby's birth while in the company of other people. I would have to leave and go far away. I would have to live alone.

It should have been a happy day. I had grown, but all I could think was, *I am growing. I am growing crazy.*

# CHAPTER TWENTY-FOUR
## Where There's a Will, There's No Way

I decided I wouldn't have to leave right away. Babies take a long time to be born, almost a year. So I could wait.

As the summer heat cooled and the leaves began to turn yellow and orange and red, my aunts traveled to the markets in turn. They traded their yarns and cloth and tapestries for grain and potatoes and carrots and onions. Ida came back with a bushel of apples and a pot of honey, which Hadel thought was very foolish, but even she couldn't hide her delight at eating apple pies and hot biscuits drizzled with honey.

I licked my lips at the sight of all the food stacked in piles for winter. I thought I had time to stay through the winter.

One morning, when the first frost appeared, Hadel asked me to help her with a chore. She rarely even spoke to me, so I found it strange that she would ask for my help, but the chore she wanted help with was even stranger.

"It's time to move the pixie nests."

"Pixie nests? *Move* them?"

"Want to get the pixies out just before they're ready to sleep for the winter so they're too tired to move back."

"Why don't you just move them when they're sleeping?"

"Have you ever woken a pixie from its winter sleep? Foolish thing to do. We move them while they're tired but not sleeping."

I watched as Hadel hobbled around and picked up what looked like nothing more than a decaying log, but when she brought it close, I peeked inside and saw a swarm of pixies crawling around, a hundred at least. They yawned and cuddled against each other or wrapped themselves in leaves, feathers, and bits of wool. They didn't seem to notice or care that they were being carried off.

If only I had known about this before, I could have moved all the pixies far away from the cottage and the mines. Spring on The Mountain would have been a much more pleasant time.

"Hold this," said Hadel. "I will gather others and you will follow me to where we will leave them." She placed the nest gently in my arms and then hobbled off to gather other nests. She picked up a bundle of twigs and grass and reached up into the branches of a tree and brought down a tangled mass. This one looked like a bird's nest, only woven completely shut in a delicate sphere. Another nest was made of leaves and twigs that hung like a basket from a tree. She cradled the nests in her apron.

I looked down at the log-nest in my arms. A pixie had fluttered sleepily to the opening. It chirped and sniffed like a squirrel searching for food. It fluttered its wings and landed on my hand. Oh no. Another came and another, until half the nest had risen from their sleepy stupor and were crawling up and down my arms and head, chirping and squeaking. One pixie with bright orange hair crawled down my nose, wrapped his hands around my nostril, and looked inside. His wings tickled my nose. I sneezed, and all the pixies shrieked and swarmed around me. Soon they settled again and continued their exploration.

Hadel came around a tree and froze at the sight of me.

"I think it would have been better to wait until they were really asleep," I said.

"Stay still!" she hissed.

"I am."

"Don't move."

"I'm not."

"Stop talking!"

I shut my mouth.

With one hand, Hadel untied her apron and gently placed the nests on the ground. She took a bucket and filled it with dirt and walked slowly toward me. "I'm going to pour this on you, but don't move until I say, understand? Don't answer. Don't move, don't even blink."

Of course I needed to blink. My eyes burned and my nose started to itch. I think I needed to sneeze again. And now my eyes were watering. Hadel walked slowly toward me. Painfully slow. Tears ran down my cheeks and the pixies swarmed on my face. The sneeze was burning in my nose. I tried to hold it in, but that only made it worse. I exploded.

"Ah–CHOO!"

Hadel pounced on me and flipped the bucket on top of me. The dirt poured down my head and face and arms.

The pixies scattered and screamed. Hadel took their nest and pulled out the bits of wool and leaves and made a trail for them, leading the pixies away from me to the hollow log. Slowly, the pixies calmed, gathered their bedding, and flew back into the nest.

As soon as the pixies had settled, Hadel hobbled to me, her wide eye boring into mine. "Has that ever happened before?"

Of course it had happened before. Pixies were always pestering me. But Hadel already suspected that something wasn't right with me, and I wasn't about to give her any more reason to think so.

"No," I said. "Pixies usually hate me."

"Do they?" She seemed amused. "Pixies have always been abundant here. They like shiny things, pretty things, but their numbers seem to be even greater since you arrived. Like they smell what they really love. *Gold.*"

"Gold?" I said, as though I had never heard of this before.

"Yes, gold. They can smell it from far away, and deep down in the earth. They smell it like a wolf smells blood, Robert." She lowered her one big eye right level with mine. My heart was beating very hard in my chest so I could hear it pounding in my ears.

"My name isn't Robert," I said quietly. "My mother, she didn't ever get to say my whole name before she died. No one ever heard all of it, you see. The only part she said was 'Rump.'" I laughed nervously, but Hadel didn't. She only widened her big eye. She knew what the name was really supposed to be. Tears burned in my eyes. I didn't want to cry, not now in front of Hadel. I held my breath until the burning stopped.

"So you've spun, have you?" asked Hadel. Her voice was a little softer now.

I nodded.

"Spun yourself into trouble?"

"A wi— My friend's granny told me that there was a way to get out of it. She said I needed a stiltskin."

"A stiltskin," mused Hadel. "Yes, I've heard of them. Very rare, mysterious magic. I've never seen one. But, yes . . . maybe. Still, even with a stiltskin, it would be difficult."

"Is there anything else? Is there any other help for it?"

Hadel put her knobby hand on my shoulder and pressed down. "There's only one thing I know for sure about spinning."

I waited, my whole chest expanding with hope.

"When you get your wool tangled in a knot, only the tangler can get it untangled."

And with that, she scooped up her apron of pixie nests and hobbled away. She did not ask me to help.

"Is something wrong, Robert? You look pale." Ida brushed her hands on my cheek. "You didn't eat. Are you ill?"

"Just tired."

"Too tired to eat?"

Hadel glanced up at me but didn't say anything. She didn't tell Ida or Balthilda about my name, and somehow this made me feel more hopeless, as if there was no need to explain because there was nothing they could do.

Ida sent me to bed early, but no sleep came. I waited for my aunts to settle in, and once I heard their even breathing and snores, I crept into the wool room with a handful of straw. The spinning wheel shone in a sliver of moonlight. I sat down. It was just a bunch of wood. In my hands was straw. Straw and wood, plain and totally unmagical. I tried to feel the magic in the air. I lifted my hands and closed my eyes and pictured pushing all the magic away. Back into the earth or the sun or wherever it came from.

> *Straw is straw*
> *Gold is gold*
> *This straw I hold*
> *Won't turn to gold*

I started pushing down on the treadle, and I fed the straw through the wheel. *Straw is straw. Gold is . . .*

Gold. The straw turned to gold. I broke off the strand of gold and wrapped it around my finger. I tried again. Straw, straw, straw.

Gold. I ripped off the thread and crushed it to a tiny ball. I would not let the rumpel overpower me!

By my feet was Hadel's wool basket. I took a handful of wool. Maybe straw always turned to gold, but I could spin wool without magic.

> *Wool is dull*
> *Wool is old*
> *No dull wool*
> *Can shine like gold*

I spun with raging speed. If I was fast enough, maybe the magic wouldn't have time to work. I saw a gray strand emerge from the wheel. My heart skipped a beat. It wasn't changing! Then the dull gray lightened and shimmered, and before my very eyes it transformed into a thick, shining thread, stretched tight over the wheel. Gold.

There were rocks in my throat. I broke the thread off quickly and jumped away from the wheel, like somehow I had infected it with my curse.

I went back to bed with the gold threads wound tightly around my finger, making it numb and tingly. I thought of my mother, holding me at birth, whispering my name in my ear.

*Rumpel . . .*

Trapped. Tangled. Ensnared. But why? Why would a mother who loved her child bestow such a fate upon him? I wanted there to be more, another explanation, but the more I thought about it, the more trapped and tangled I felt, and I knew that there was nothing more. Only the cruel echo of my name.

*Rumpel, Rumpel, Rumpel.*

# CHAPTER TWENTY-FIVE

## Warnings from Red

In a week the world was white with the first snow. My aunts huddled in the wool room near the fire with their work. I didn't want to be around any of that, so I took a walk to the village. Gnomes waddled around with their tongues out, trying to catch snowflakes. That reminded me painfully of Red. I scooped up a girl gnome with pigtails and a pudgy nose. "This message is for Red in The Mountain."

"Message for Red in The Mountain!" she squealed.

I hadn't gotten a message from Red since I came to live with my aunts. I was a little worried. Was she all right? I wanted to talk to her, but with the gnome wriggling in my arms, I found I didn't know what to say.

Dear Red,
  I'm living with my three aunts, who are witches. My real name is Rumpel, and it means

> I'm trapped in magic forever and no one can
> help me. Opal is having a baby, and I might
> have to take it.

I just didn't think that message would inspire Red to respond. Mostly, I wanted to send her something so she would send a message back.

> Dear Red,
>     I'm in Yonder now. It's not so cold here, and guess what? I have three aunts! And guess what else? I grew! Maybe I'm taller than you now. Also they call me Robert here, so it's probably better if you do too.
>                                    Your friend,
>                                    Robert

The gnome scurried down the road until she was just a speck in all the white.

After that I walked to the village every day, even though it would be at least a week before a gnome came back with a message.

It took sixteen days. The gnome was so frozen I had to take him home and thaw him in front of the fire before he could say anything to me. I was delighted at first, but then Red's message wasn't so cheerful.

> Dear Robert,
>     Lord Greedy-Fatty-Miller-Oswald is withholding more rations because we're finding even less gold. I

think the king has found Opal out. Don't worry, I won't say a thing about you-know-what. Obviously, Opal can't make gold out of straw, but the king can't kill her because . . . you know . . . , and so the king has turned his wrath on The Mountain, demanding more gold. But there is no gold. So everyone is really hungry and grumpy.

Red

P.S. You might be taller than me, but I can still pound you.

So King Barf was punishing The Mountain through "Lord" Oswald. How he must have raged when he discovered Opal couldn't really spin the gold! Maybe she told the king about me to spare herself. Maybe soldiers were already searching for me. No. That couldn't be. It had been too long. Opal and the miller were probably afraid to tell the king that they had deceived him. They must have come up with an explanation for why she couldn't spin the straw into gold anymore, like expecting a baby takes away her magic powers. Yes, I could believe that. But I wasn't too confident that Opal would think to say it.

Poor Red! She sounded so miserable. Maybe I could cheer her up with a rhyme, but the gnome who brought Red's message ran away as fast as he could from my message. I guess even gnomes have their limits. I found another in the village and sent Red a poem.

I know a miller
Greedy and fat
Smells like a troll

Looks like a rat
He steals all the gold
And he creeps like a cat
But one day The Mountain
Fell down on him
SPLAT!

I waited seven days and then went to the village every day to search for a gnome from Red. Sixteen days. Seventeen. Eighteen. I told myself it was because of the snow and ice. Maybe the gnomes refused to take any more messages such a long distance.

Twenty days.

Twenty-five days.

Thirty-four days! It took thirty-four days to get a reply, and her message was even less cheerful than the last. She didn't say anything about my poem.

Dear Robert,

The miller has been asking me about you. He asked if I knew where you were or if I'd heard from you. I wanted to punch his nosey nose, but I can't do that, so later I punched Frederick for no good reason. Well, he's Frederick. That's a reason.

Don't send a gnome back. I think the miller is starting to sniff with his oversized nose.

Your friend,

Red

P.S. As always, Granny says watch your step.

The miller was asking about me. I tried to swallow the hard lump that had risen in my throat. He couldn't possibly find me here, could he? I was far away in Yonder, tucked in a little wood with three witches who were my aunts. I was safe. Wasn't I?

But what if the miller could find me? I didn't want to believe it was possible, but if he could, I feared what he would do. He could hurt my aunts, or use them just as he'd used me. Staying with them this long had been selfish on my part. I was putting them in danger, and they deserved nothing but kindness from me.

I should probably leave now.

# CHAPTER TWENTY-SIX

## Destiny Calls

I was not safe, and neither was anyone who cared about me. I tried to brush off the feeling, especially when I sat with my aunts in the warmth of their home, eating their good food, and watching their magical spinning and knitting and weaving. But it was no use. The more I tried to tell myself not to worry, the more I worried and knew that I had to leave.

I left my aunts on a frigid morning without so much as a goodbye. I couldn't risk them knowing where I was headed, and I didn't think I could bear the looks on their faces, especially Ida. I would miss her most. I would miss our rhymes. I made up a farewell rhyme as I walked away.

*Home is a place with three dear aunts*
*They cook good food and sew nice pants*
*They spin and knit and weave and mend*
*Goodbye for now, my three dear friends*

I walked through the forest while it was still dark. My satchel weighed down on my shoulder, heavy with the food I had stolen from my aunts. My stomach was heavy with guilt.

The frozen snow crunched beneath my feet. I had decided I would go to the mountains beyond Beyond. It was the farthest place from The Kingdom that I knew of. I could live all alone, in a mountain cave far away from anyone, and herd goats and live off their milk and whatever the land would give me. I had considered going back to the trolls, thinking they might be able to protect me from my own magic. But I wasn't too fond of the idea of eating sludge for the rest of my life. My stomach wriggled at the thought. Besides, they were so close to The Kingdom, and I knew they got news of weddings and babies. The risk was too great.

I emerged from the trees and was on the road before dawn. The air was bitter cold, and I wrapped myself tighter inside the thick coat my aunts had made me. Soon I'd left the village behind.

Before long I heard muffled voices in the distance. It was still dark, but I could just make out the shadowy movements of something farther up the road. I veered off into the trees. It might just be a farmer bringing wool to the village, or a peddler coming to trade his trinkets and treasures, but I didn't want anyone to see me. As they drew nearer, their voices became clear.

"I don't think this is right," said a boy's voice. It was irritatingly familiar.

"The woman said he came this way," said another voice, also familiar.

"But she didn't see the gnome! We were supposed to be following the gnome! If you hadn't lost it—"

"It's impossible to keep up with a gnome, you idiot! And, anyway, it doesn't matter. We're on his trail. When I find that Butt, I'm going to punch him so hard he sees pixies!"

"You punch like a girl, Frederick."

"Quiet! If we don't find him, Father's going to make us go back to The Mountain and work in the mines. Do you want that?"

"No."

A chill ran down my spine that had nothing to do with the freezing air. My heart began to thump in my chest. Frederick and Bruno were standing just feet away from me. I shifted nervously, and a dead twig snapped beneath my boot.

"Shhh! Did you hear that?"

"Probably a rabbit."

I held very still. Frederick moved in my direction. If he came any closer, I would need to run. I stepped back, bracing myself.

This is where I would like to really complain about The Witch of The Woods's advice. You see, if you're going to give someone advice, it's important to be specific. *Watch your step* is not specific at all. You take a lot of steps every day, so it would really help to know *which* step to be careful on! Watch your step when you're around poop, or a trap. Watch your step when you're near a tower window. Or a pixie nest!

I stepped on a pixie nest.

I think my aunt Hadel's advice was also lacking. Waking one pixie from its winter sleep is foolish. Waking a nest full of pixies is a death wish.

A piercing shriek exploded from the ground and filled the air so that it must have reached every ear within a mile. Pixies shot out and pelted toward me like a thousand tiny arrows, pink and blue and red and orange sparks, their teeth bared for war. I screamed like a mountain lion and fell to the ground and rolled, throwing mud and dirt all over, but those pixies bit my nose, my cheeks, my ears, and all ten of my fingers. They bit clear through my clothes on my arms and legs. Three went up my pants and bit me right on my namesake.

Finally, the pixies flew away through the trees, either satisfied that they had punished me enough or tired of the dirt. I could feel all my body parts beginning to swell. My bottom expanded beneath me. My legs felt like fat logs floating on water, just bobbing around without any control. My face puffed up, making my skin stretch and tighten. Although my eyes were swollen nearly shut, I could see enough to know that Frederick and Bruno were standing over me. They wore soldiers' uniforms and both pointed big hunting knives right at my face.

"Hello, Butt," said Frederick. "Fancy a stroll?"

"No thank you, I'm rather busy" is what I meant to say, but that's not what came out through my swollen lips.

It was more like "No shaksoo, I sathoo bithy," and drool ran down my face.

Frederick laughed. "I didn't think you could get any uglier. Tie him up."

Bruno knelt down and grabbed my puffy hands to tie them together. He had a time of it, though. My hands were so fat it was almost impossible to get my wrists together. Finally, he tied me at the elbows, which was probably the only place the pixies didn't bite.

"We've missed you so much, Butt," said Frederick, and he patted my swollen face. I winced.

Bruno laughed. "Father misses you too, and so does our sister, the queen."

I was afraid they were going to tell me she'd had the baby, but they didn't. I breathed. As long as she didn't have a baby or I didn't hear of it, there was a way out of this. Of course the miller wanted me to spin gold for him, but I didn't have to. I wouldn't. Not for anything!

They dragged me out of the trees and then marched me down the road, in the direction I had already been traveling, but definitely not where I wanted to go. I knew this was a very serious problem. Frederick and Bruno were kidnapping me at knifepoint. I should have been terrified. But I couldn't think of any of that because I was seething mad at that swarm of pixies and at Red's granny for her vague advice. I had sausage fingers, I could barely see, I was drooling out of fat lips, and my butt was lopsided. It's very awkward to walk with a lopsided bottom.

As I waddled down the road, my heart swelled too—

with sadness. I could say that none of it mattered, that I should just give up and let the tangles keep wrapping until they covered the top of my head and pushed me down into the earth. What did it matter that Frederick and Bruno had captured me? What did it matter that they were taking me to the miller, who wanted me to spin him gold forever? But in my heart it mattered. I didn't want to be trapped. I wanted to grow. I wanted to break free.

When the sun set, we stopped to camp, and I was tied to a tree near the road. I was actually grateful to sit on snow and ice. It soothed my sore, sorry rump. But I was also starving, and I watched hungrily as Frederick and Bruno tore through my satchel and ate all the food I had packed. They threw me a chunk of bread, which I had to bend down and eat in the dirt like a dog.

Frederick commanded Bruno to guard me. When they were together, Bruno did whatever his brother told him, but by himself he was meaner than Frederick. Maybe he was only mean to me because other people made him feel small and he wanted to prove that he was big. I suddenly felt sorry for Bruno in a way I never had, and Frederick too, because he probably felt small around the miller and the miller probably felt small around someone else, like King Barf. But I didn't feel too sorry. Bruno might feel smaller than me even, but I didn't think meanness was ever in anyone's destiny. Meanness was a choice.

At first we only sat in silence, but then Bruno grew bored. He laughed and poked my swollen face.

"They made a good breakfast of you, didn't they?"

He laughed and laughed until he fell in the snow and sputtered at the cold shock.

As darkness fell, it grew very cold. I sat shivering against the tree, while Frederick wrapped himself in a thick woolen blanket. Bruno tried to do the same, but Frederick yanked his blanket away. "Keep watching Butt," he commanded.

"He's tied up tight enough," whined Bruno.

"I said watch him!"

Bruno faced me and glowered, but as soon as Frederick was asleep, he wrapped himself in his blanket and curled up by the fire.

"Good night, Butt!" Bruno whispered loudly, and then joined his brother in snoring slumber.

I waited and shivered. Everything was quiet. The fire was dead, and there was only a sliver of moonlight to see by. It was impossible to sleep because I was so cold and swollen with pixie bites. So I stayed awake thinking about my destiny, and when I got tired of that, I cursed pixies and gnomes, but mostly pixies.

But then a miracle happened. During the night, my swelling started to go down, helped by the cold air, I guess, and as it went down, my bindings loosened. I wriggled but it wasn't quite enough to get me free.

I deflated a little more every hour, and I wriggled and wriggled as Frederick and Bruno snored on. Just as the sky was fading from black to purple, my hands and arms were almost back to normal and they slipped out of the ropes.

I praised the pixies. I wished they had bitten me a

hundred more times and made me as fat as the miller. Beautiful, lovely pixies! It's funny how some things you think are so terrible can turn out to be really wonderful. I loved my swollen arms and fingers and my lopsided butt!

Something rustled in the bushes. Probably just a squirrel or a rabbit, but it made Bruno stop snoring. He smacked his lips and pulled his covers tighter around him.

I moved as fast and as quietly as I could. With my arms free, I was able to wriggle myself out of the rest of the ropes. Just as I pulled the last rope over my head, the rustling noise came again, and from the shrubs appeared a gnome. He was hopping with great excitement.

"Greetings from The Kingdom! King Barfy-hew Archy-baldy Regy-naldy Fife and Queen Opal both happily announce the birth of their new son, heir to the throne of The Kingdom. His name is—"

I clamped my hand over the gnome's mouth, but it was too late. I had heard exactly what I didn't want to hear, and Frederick and Bruno were awake now, staring bleary-eyed between the gnome and me.

I dropped the gnome, scrambled to my feet, and ran. Except I ran in exactly the opposite direction from where I wished to go. I had freed myself from Frederick and Bruno's ropes, but the ropes that had been tangled and knotted inside of me were now tugging at me—pulling me like a stubborn donkey in the direction of The Kingdom.

It was time to collect on my worst bargain ever.

# CHAPTER TWENTY-SEVEN

## The Miller and the Merchant

It is a very strange feeling to have your brain doing one thing and your body doing something else. It was like my mind was attached to some bizarre creature and it was carrying me away captive.

Soon Frederick and Bruno caught up with me, and for the rest of our journey they led me by a rope like a cow, but I hardly noticed. Rumpel is tighter than any real rope. It can't be cut or loosened. My legs would have carried me over the bridge and up the hill and to the walls of the castle. They probably would have carried me right through walls and through fire and spears to get to Opal, so powerless was I against this magic, but with Frederick and Bruno, it was all too easy. When we reached the castle, the guards saluted them and opened the gates.

We crossed the grounds, entered the castle doors, now gilded gold, marched up a grand golden staircase, and down a long corridor to a large golden door with gold handles. Frederick knocked and we went in.

The room was smaller than I expected. In the center stood a cradle, covered in white satin and embroidered with gold thread. Opal hovered over the cradle. She looked very different from the last time I saw her. Her eyes were no longer blank, but sunken with exhaustion. She was pale and thin, and her golden hair was loose and disheveled. I guess being a queen and a mother makes you worried and tired—not to mention the added worry of your baby being taken away.

The cradle began to wail, and Opal reached inside to pick up her baby and hold him close to her chest. She shook and her eyes brimmed with tears as she saw me watching. "Please . . ."

I opened my mouth to say that I didn't want her baby. I just wanted to get away and never make another promise as long as I lived. But I couldn't. My tongue swelled in my mouth. I couldn't say anything against the bargain.

"Well, well, well," said another voice beside me. "Our little man has returned to make good on your promise." It was Oswald the miller, fatter than ever, his girth covered in red velvet, trimmed with gold threads. He looked like a giant tomato ready to burst.

"Now, daughter, give the little man what you promised," he said, his voice so oily it slithered.

Opal clenched her jaw and stiffened, clearly trying to fight her father's command. But something prevented her—the magic. The same magic that commanded me. She was fighting just like I was against the invisible ropes that pulled me toward the baby. When I had spun her the gold, Opal had laughed at the idea of giving me her first-born child. She hadn't taken the promise seriously, or perhaps she hadn't considered what it meant to be a mother, how she would love her child. She had thought it a good joke. I'd never imagined she would make such a foolish promise. We had both been fools. I didn't want her baby and she didn't want to give it to me. What was the point of a bargain neither person wanted to keep? But the magic was closing in on both of us. We had no choice now.

"I knew you would go to her," said the miller, "after the king took her away. I didn't worry because I knew you would spin the gold and Opal could give you anything in return. Anything, and the gold would be hers." He laughed, his whole body jiggling. "Oh, but her unborn child! Her unborn child! Well, I suppose this will teach her not to make such rash promises. Now, daughter, give him what you promised. Give him the child."

I unwillingly took a step forward, and Opal shook as she tried to back away from me, but couldn't. We were just a few steps apart. Opal clutched her infant tighter still.

"Don't come near me or I'll scream! I'll scream and they'll break down the door and you'll be dragged into the dungeon or put in the stocks or hanged!"

The miller laughed. "Don't talk nonsense, silly girl. What would the king say were he to learn that you never really spun the gold, but bargained his child to this . . . creature? This little demon?"

Demon? I'd been called many things, but demon? That felt a bit harsh.

"You've already fallen out of favor with him," Oswald continued, "but give over the child and we can make things right. He will be forgiving of your carelessness if he has the gold. He'd rather have the gold than a child."

Would he, really? People often said that the king loved gold more than anything, but certainly not more than his own son, his heir.

"No! No, he wouldn't. He loves our son!" Opal protested.

"It doesn't matter," said the miller. "You made a promise. He spun you the gold. The child is his."

I saw then that the miller understood the magic. It was like he could see the invisible ropes pulling at me. He knew—perhaps he had known all along—that I had to take the baby, that I had no control. But there was something else in his eyes, a malicious pleasure, as if he were enjoying the suffering. And it was only the beginning. He wanted me to take the baby so he could inflict more pain.

The miller clasped his hands over his belly. "Now, let's get on with it, shall we? We have much more interesting things to discuss than babies."

The invisible ropes pulled tighter, and this time Opal was the one who stepped forward. If I reached my arms out, I would be able to touch the baby. Opal was trembling. "I'll give you all the riches in The Kingdom. Anything you want. Please don't take my baby."

The miller scoffed. "He *gave* you all the riches you have." I hated to admit it, but he had a point. "And you shall have plenty more children when we are through, only take care not to bargain them away." The miller's voice turned harsh and cold. "Give him the child, girl."

"Please!" Opal broke down and cried, each breath coming out in racking sobs. I was filled with pity for her. I fought as hard as I could against my next step. I thought of my own mother, holding me close as she whispered my name in my ear. Had she meant to bestow such a mean fate upon me? Did she want for me to be tangled in all this magic? All because of a name. A name is supposed to be your destiny, it's supposed to give you power, but I was utterly powerless. My name told me I was, and I didn't see how I could change that.

Opal was before me now, kneeling and holding her baby to me. He was fast asleep, a tiny creature. Luckily, he looked nothing like his father.

"What is his name?" I asked.

"Archie," she whispered. "Archibald Bartholomew Oswald." And she sobbed more after saying the last two names. I couldn't blame her.

I took the baby from her arms, and Opal slumped to the ground, wetting the wood planks with her tears. Here I held the future king in my arms. He started to squirm and make noise. What was I supposed to do when it made noise?

"Good," said the miller. "Now that bargains have been kept and promises fulfilled, I think it best that we move on. Yes, little demon, we have business to discuss."

The miller's eyes were now overflowing with an insatiable greed. I looked away in disgust, and suddenly I realized why the room felt so small. Straw. Walls of straw, mountains of straw. It towered on both sides of the room, covering all the walls to the ceiling. There was only a narrow space from the door to the center of the room, where the cradle lay, and then a small clearing behind that for the window. To my right, the straw was cleared for the fireplace. In front of the fireplace was a spinning wheel. A chill ran down my spine and I shivered.

"No," I said. *Never again!*

"Oh, come, come," said Oswald. "I think you rather enjoy making the gold. Gives you a feeling of power, usefulness. Your mother felt the same." He grinned wickedly.

"My mother? But you . . . she . . ."

"Oh yes," he said. "I knew of her gift. I met her long before she came to The Mountain. I believe I was the first to benefit from her skill, as I shall be the last. How delighted I was to learn that these things can be passed on."

My insides went cold. The floor tilted beneath me. "You're the merchant," I said. "You're the one who made her spin all that straw into gold."

"No, no, I never *made* her. I believe she was rather enthusiastic, and we always struck a bargain. It was always a fair trade. Straw isn't worth all that much, you know. I was rather generous, really." He rubbed his immense belly.

"But then she ran away to that blasted mountain. Thought she could hide there in all the gold, but I caught up to her—and a good thing too. Provident, even. The miller had just died with no sons to carry on his work. I was wealthy enough to buy the mill, and I think your mother was glad in the end. I daresay you're alive because

I kept her so well fed after your father died. And aren't you grateful? You probably wouldn't have been born had I not bargained with her, the poor soul. It's a pity she died." He gave out a long, exaggerated sigh.

"But I did hope that her son might show a bit of the same promise. So I waited. I was patient, and you did not disappoint. Frederick and Bruno were charged to keep an eye on you, and how delighted I was when my sons came and told me the outlandish story that you had a pile of gold in your cottage.

"It was all too easy to get you to come begging, and then you became quite greedy. Wanted more food than everyone else. You didn't even share. Shameful. And then we had the blunder with the king! Yes, he's a bit more attentive than his predecessor when it comes to the gold being traded in his kingdom. I should have known. . . . Ah, well, things turned out better than I had hoped, what with you spinning for Opal. And now she is the queen."

Opal remained curled on the ground, sobbing.

"But we are not through. You see, little demon, though Opal is the queen and I am Lord of The Mountain, the king is not pleased with her lack of performance these past months. Of course we have made our excuses with her delicate situation, but that has all passed. And so it has become necessary that we please our king, and perhaps ourselves, a little more." He chuckled, running his hands over the straw.

I hated him. Rage gathered in my stomach, burned in my chest, making my head throb. *He* was the demon. He was the reason for my mother's sorrow, her entrapment, and her death. All my troubles had begun with the miller. "I'm not spinning any more gold," I said.

"Really?" said the miller, amused.

The baby began to cry in my arms, and Opal wailed too.

"I think I've got all I can handle. Thanks." I backed away. He could hold me here forever, but there was nothing he could offer me that would make me spin a single straw into gold. Nothing!

"But you haven't heard what I have to offer," he said, grinning wickedly.

A chill ran down my spine. I just knew it was going to be something awful.

"I don't want anything. I'm not spinning." I started to back away with the baby in my arms. Better to stop here. Just take the baby and leave. But Frederick and Bruno grabbed my arms on either side and held fast.

"Oh, I think you'll reconsider in a moment," said the miller. "It's such a good bargain. For your gold, I shall give you . . ." He reached behind a stack of straw, and the whole pile shook, as though an animal was struggling to get out.

". . . I shall give you your friend unharmed."

The miller pulled a girl from out of the straw, bound and gagged. One of her eyes was black and swollen, but the other was wide, burning with a fierce and savage rage.

Red.

# CHAPTER TWENTY-EIGHT

## Grasping at Straws

Red fought against her bindings and gave a muffled scream beneath the gag until she was purple.

The miller laughed. "She is a feisty one, I'll say. Rather impolite. It took both Frederick and Bruno to catch her. They told me she was your only friend in the world, and, well . . . I suppose if you have only one friend, you might want to keep her. In one piece, that is."

Frederick and Bruno laughed, and Red flailed and struggled against the ropes. Frederick and Bruno stopped laughing and stepped back. Even though she was bound, Red was like a mad beast that might break free at any moment.

"Boys," said the miller, "set our little friend in the corner. Then go find a place to wash. You smell like swine."

Frederick and Bruno shoved Red into the corner by the fireplace and then left.

"Now," said the miller, turning to me. "Do we have a bargain?" Red made a muffled growl and shook her head behind Oswald. What did she think I should do? I couldn't let her get hurt.

The baby in my arms had been squirming and whimpering all this while, but suddenly he exploded in shrill wails. He sounded like a whole swarm of mad pixies.

"He's hungry! Let me have him!" cried Opal, rushing toward me, but the miller stopped her. "Not until he starts spinning."

Spinning, spinning, spinning. Red and gold and Opal and the baby. I couldn't think with all the wailing! I would have to think while I spun.

"Take him and feed him!" I shouted to Opal, and sat down at the spinning wheel. My hands shook as I picked up the straw. The spinning wheel vibrated when I put my foot on the treadle, like it knew something bad was happening. This was the sort of magic Hadel had warned me about. It was *wrong*. Twisted. I pushed the straw through the wheel and began to spin.

"Very wise," said Oswald. "Now, the king grows impatient. He is eager for his queen to display her talents once again, and as you can see, he's gathered straw all this time, just for her to spin. You have three days."

"Three days?" I asked. "I can't finish this in three days!"

"In three days the king will return with his hunting party," said the miller. "We have promised him results. Therefore you will promise to make the gold. Three days. Fail me, and the bargain is off." He smiled malevolently at Red. She glared at him. Anger welled up in me stronger than I had ever felt it before. I wanted to punch him—punch him in his big red belly and make him explode! And then the anger faded into despair. I was back where I started. Three days would not be the end. I would never stop spinning the straw into gold. Gran had tried to keep me from all this, from the miller and his greed, from my own stupidity, but maybe there was nothing either of us could have done.

The miller stepped forward with a length of rope and bound my legs and ankles to the spinning wheel. "We wouldn't want you to get lost," he said.

No, I couldn't be lost. My name was Rumpel. I was trapped.

One spool of gold.

Red was sitting on the floor. She was dirtier than I'd ever seen her. She had scratches and cuts, and the dirt on her face was streaked as though she had been crying. Red crying. Strong, fierce, fearless Red, crying. I hated to imagine.

Two spools of gold.

Opal sat in a pile of straw, feeding her baby. She was crying too. When she finished, the miller made her put Archie in a basket next to me and told her to back away, to remind us both that he was mine. Some grandfather.

Three spools of gold. Four.

The miller gathered the gold as I spun it, draping it around his neck and waist, and laughing all the while.

Finally, after he was more tangled in gold than Red was in rope, he slumped down and his head began to nod. I was feeling hopeful. If he fell asleep, I could untie Red and we could make a run for it, but then I remembered Archie. Even if I could free myself, I would have to take the baby and Opal would probably start shrieking and that would be that. But I wanted to at least talk to Red.

"Opal," I said after the miller started snoring. "Ungag Red." Opal looked at me as if I had insulted her. I tried to sound more submissive and pleading.

"Your Highness, please? Take off Red's gag?"

"No," she said sharply. "*I'm* the queen, and you don't give me orders. She's a mean creature. She always pulled my hair when I was a girl. Evil, that's what she is. Red is *evil.*"

Red gave Opal a look that could certainly be called evil, and Opal cowered and then lashed out at me. "And so are you, you little demon baby stealer!" She began to wail again. Oh, make it stop! I couldn't think! I needed Red's brains right now. Mine were just too scrambled.

"Opal, Your Majesty. If you let her speak to me, I may be able to tell you a way that you can keep your baby." It was a hollow promise, but I knew it would work for now. Opal stopped crying and her eyes widened.

"My baby? You'll give him back . . . ? For good?"

"I can tell you how it might be possible if you take off Red's gag."

Opal obeyed, and as soon as she did, Red let out a slew of curses that I didn't think appropriate for infant ears. The baby didn't either, because he started crying and the miller began to stir in his sleep. Quickly, Opal picked up Archie and rocked and soothed him, which soothed the sleeping miller as well. I had to admit, seeing Opal cuddle and whisper to her baby was very sweet. It made my heart pinch and swell all at once. I really didn't want to take her baby.

"Rump, you idiot," said Red in a harsh whisper, "why did you come back?"

"I didn't want to," I said, still spinning the straw. "Frederick and Bruno found me and kidnapped me, and I almost got away until a gnome found me and announced the birth of Opal's baby. Then I had to come. Did you know that magic can force you to do something you don't want to?"

"Magic will make you do anything you've bound your-self to," said Red. "Why do you think witches don't like to get involved in anything? You're in a tangle, Rump."

Since birth.

"Well, what about you? Unless I spin this gold, you're going to die."

"And what do you think they'll do with you? Make you lord of the pixies? Oh, please, Rump! *You're* the one who's going to die if you *don't* stop!"

"I can't. Red, I can't." In a whisper, I quickly told her what I had learned about my aunts and my mother and my name. Her eyes widened as I spoke, and when I finished, all she managed to say was "Oh."

The things I'd said hung in the air for a heavy moment.

"This is my destiny, Red. I don't have any choice."

"That's not true, Rump. You do have a choice."

I started to feel irritated. "I *don't* have a choice, Red, unless I choose to let the miller hurt you, maybe even *kill* you. Or kill me. Do you want me to make that choice?"

"No, Rump! That's not what I—"

The miller snorted and sat up abruptly, looking dazed and confused. "Wha . . . ? What are you . . . ?"

Red whispered frantically to me. "Your name, Rump. There has to be more than that. Your mother wouldn't have done that!"

"You think you know so much. There isn't more! My destiny is *this*!"

The miller came to his senses. He grabbed a handful of Red's hair, and she growled and struggled against him.

"Rump! This isn't your destiny! You're not—" The miller fastened the gag over her mouth again and threw her against a pile of straw so forcefully that a heap fell over her head and buried her up to her chest. Oswald glowered at her and she glowered back. Then he walked slowly over to me.

I concentrated on spinning, hunched low as I fed the straw into the wheel. *Whir, whir, whir.* Another spool. A little pile had formed at my feet. The miller's massive shadow fell over me. He bent down close and I could smell his breath. It smelled like rotting meat and sour ale, worse than a troll's breath.

"Do something like that again and I'll put your little friend in a haystack and set it on fire." His hand came down across my face and knocked me back from the wheel. Straw flew everywhere, like thick golden rain. "Get up. You will not stop until every last bit of straw is gold."

He turned to Opal, who was clutching her baby, protecting him from her father's fury. "You, put that thing back in the basket. It doesn't belong to you."

Opal obeyed. I obeyed.

I spun in silence for many hours. The afternoon sun burned through the window, making the spools of gold glow red. I had a good high stack, but I didn't think I had put a dent in all the straw. I would have to spin through the night if I was to finish in three days, and one of the days was nearly gone. I was already exhausted.

When the sun was low in the sky, Frederick and Bruno took me outside so that I could relieve myself of nature's call. They stood right by me, their hands on the big knives at their waists, reminding me that I was trapped. At least the cold air revived me a little and I could think more clearly. I forced my brain not to think about my destiny or myself. I thought only of getting Red out of this mess. Whatever problems I had, she didn't deserve to be tangled up in them. I would get her free, and then I'd deal with everything else.

Back in the castle, the miller tied me to the wheel again and stood over me as I spun. Whenever I filled the bobbin, he quickly removed the skein and added it to the growing pile of gold. Opal had scooted as near to Archie as she dared, looking back and forth between her father and me. She drew her legs up to her chest and wrapped her arms tightly around her shins and rocked back and forth, in rhythm to my spinning. She rocked so vigorously that the floorboards beneath her began to creak. By nightfall the boards lifted each time she rocked back and then cracked down as she came forward. *Creak, snap! Creak, snap!*

Red stared at me as I spun, a look of hard determination on her face. I shrugged helplessly, and she rolled her eyes and sank back into the straw. I didn't dare talk. My face still burned from the miller's hand. But questions tumbled around in my head. A thousand little birds pecking at my brains. Red said I hadn't found all my name. But how did that help me? Even if it was true, I was no closer to finding out the rest. And, besides, *Rumpel* made sense. Trapped, trapped, trapped.

Eventually, the miller fell asleep in a pile of straw, and the moment he did, Opal crept over to me with a desperate look in her eyes. "You said you would tell me how I could keep my baby. Tell me now."

I stared at her. I had nearly forgotten our agreement, but Opal had been waiting all this time for the miller to fall asleep so she could ask. Her eyes were red and puffy, and her face was wet with tears. Her chin trembled, and before I could say anything, she started crying again.

"Stop! Stop, Opal. I mean, Your Majesty. There *is* a way that you can keep your baby. Stop crying!"

She stopped crying and I sighed with relief.

"Tell me," said Opal as she wiped her nose on her sleeve.

I racked my brain wildly. I looked at Red, but she just shook her head at me. We both knew there was no way, but I had to tell Opal something. Anything. I had to give her an impossible task.

"You must tell me my name," I said.

"Your name?" she asked.

"Yes, my true name. All of it. If you guess my name before I'm done spinning this gold, you can keep your baby."

"But your name is Robert," she said. "Or, no, it's Butt. Frederick and Bruno always called you Butt."

"My name has never been Robert or Butt," I said impatiently. "You have to guess my real name."

"And if I do, you'll give me back Archie?"

I nodded. I knew I was secure in this bargain. She would never guess my name. I didn't even have a real name, only a curse. "I promise."

Opal took a deep, shuddering breath. "I can speak to the king's wise men and search all the Name Books."

Whatever kept her busy and wail-free. She went off looking much lighter. But my burden was still heavy, and my legs and back already ached. I was in a sea of gold now, a filthy gold ocean.

Later, Opal strolled into the room with a list of names written on a long scroll. "Is your name Gaspar? Or Melchior? Balthasar? Those are very rare names. Is it one of those?"

I stared at her in disbelief. "Rump," I said. "My name has always started with *Rump*."

"But that can't be your real name!"

"It's only part of my name."

She looked confused and stared down at her parchment. "Is it Nebuchadnezzar?"

I stopped my spinning and stared at her. Was she serious? My sympathy for Opal was fading with the thickening of her skull.

"That is not my name."

"Oh" was all she said, and she turned away, sighing at all the work she had wasted.

Opal stared blankly at the parchment a bit longer, then stretched out and fell asleep in the straw, her arms reaching toward her sleeping baby.

As soon as Opal fell asleep, the miller snorted awake, rubbed his eyes, and grinned at all the gold. He took a large sack and began filling it with gold. "That's good," he said looking at the gold, not me. "Plenty for all." He stuffed the sack to the brim and then staggered out of the room with the bulging sack flung over his shoulder.

The first day was gone, and though the pile of gold grew above my head, the straw still loomed like a mountain.

A few pixies crawled through the cracks in the floorboards. All the gold and magic must have awakened them from their winter sleep. They danced and chirped around me and the spinning wheel for a minute and then nestled in the coils of gold and fell asleep. Buzzards. How I longed to join them.

# CHAPTER TWENTY-NINE

## Guessing Games for Finding Names

"Sheepshanks, Cruikshanks, Spindleshanks?"

I allowed Opal to rattle off any ridiculous name she wanted. The fact that my name actually began with *Rump* still hadn't gotten through. Either way it would all come to nothing, but at least it kept her from crying.

"Gibblyshanks, Woolyshanks, Peppershanks?"

The door opened and the miller entered. Opal crumpled up her list of silly names and jumped away from me, but the miller took no notice of her. He went right to the gold and started to refill his sack.

"I think we will exceed the king's expectations, even if we do not give him all the gold." He laughed wickedly as he stuffed the sack with gold. "Yes, he'll never notice the difference."

Opal glared at her father. "What makes you think you

can keep any of it? I could tell him, you know. I *am* the queen."

The miller smiled. "You could tell him, just as easily as I could tell him it was not you who spun the gold. How do you think the king would take that?"

Opal clamped her mouth shut and looked away. The miller cast his gaze on me, and I quickened my foot on the treadle. Then he left. As soon as the door had snapped shut, Opal spouted off another trio of names.

"Bindershanks, Spindershanks, Thistleshanks?" She went through a hundred "shanks" names and continued to speak to servants and messengers through the crack of the door as they handed her new lists. Some of the names made me glad I was called Rump. Who would want to name their child Peabody? I'd rather be a Rump than a Peabody.

Opal kept busy with the names, unless the miller was present, and when Archie needed feeding she seemed quite peeved to have to stop. She had become so obsessed with finding my name she forgot why she was looking for it in the first place.

In the meantime, the miller was piling the gold in little stacks and counting them. Frederick and Bruno helped him, but the miller slapped their hands if they lingered on the skeins too long. Sometimes they'd watch me spin with a kind of awe, and I almost thought they were admiring me, but their eyes were only on the gold.

Red tried to communicate with me at first, making faces and shaking her head this way and that, but after a while she gave up and sank into herself, just staring into the fire and sleeping in small stretches.

Oswald gave Red and me stale bread and moldy cheese to eat, but Red didn't eat any, and I worried. I stuffed the food in my mouth and spun faster. Even if it was vile, I needed the energy to finish my task.

Opal continued guessing names for me: "Adelbrecht, Herbercik, Zettelmeiger."

"That is not my name," I said, and continued to spin. With the *whir, whir, whir* of the wheel, I heard *Rumpel, Rumpel, Rumpel. Trapped, trapped, trapped.*

"Ferdinand! Ferdinando! Eginhard!"

"That is not my name."

Opal began to despair and my guilt deepened. I had given her false hope. Maybe I had given myself false hope, as if there really could be more to me than just a tangled mess.

*Whir, whir, whir*

*Rumpel, Rumpel, Rumpel*

*Trapped, trapped, trapped*

As the second day drew to a close, Opal rocked back and forth on the floor again, and the boards creaked and lifted.

*Creak, snap. Creak, snap. Whir, whir, whir.*

A few times I actually saw people through the cracks in the floorboards, moving around in the room below. I heard the sound of chatter and recognized a familiar voice. It was Martha, the cook who had helped me when I fell out of the tower. It was sort of funny that I was right above her now. I strained my ears to catch any good gossip she might have, but I couldn't hear well enough to make sense of it.

The gold was now stacked higher than the straw, far above my head, but heaps and heaps of straw still remained. I couldn't see the end of it. And once I finished, I knew the miller would find new ways to manipulate me.

There had to be a way out. Red had said there was a way. Her granny had said so too. There was something I was missing, I just knew it, but I couldn't see what. I couldn't think in this small space filled with straw and gold. I needed air. I needed rest. I closed my eyes and put my head down on the wheel. I would only rest for a minute.

*reak, snap. Creak, snap.*

My head jerked up at the sound. Opal was rocking back and forth again, lifting the floorboards. I looked around, dazed. Gold and straw were everywhere, and out the window I could see it was dark. I had fallen asleep. The second day was gone. How late was it?

I lifted my arms to stretch. I hadn't moved all day from the spinning wheel, not even to answer the calls of nature. Nature was screaming at me, and so was my brain. I had the strange feeling that I'd just awoken from a dream, but I couldn't remember what it was. I was thinking of destiny and names. The Witch of The Woods and stiltskins. My aunts and the rumpels. The trolls and their magical hoard. The apple tree. My mother. There were ideas flying inside my head, answers, but they couldn't get out in this room. My brain needed open space.

"I have to go outside," I announced. "Nature calls."

"Can't it wait?" said Oswald.

"I've been holding it in for a long time. I might have an accident and get it all over the straw, and I'm not sure I can make gold out of pee-straw."

The miller's eyes flashed, but he waved me away. "Frederick, Bruno. Take our friend outside. Make sure he's well protected."

The brothers sat up and smiled malevolently. They had done very little the past two days besides watch me spin gold or run mindless errands for the miller. They were restless and bored, and that was a dangerous state for Frederick and Bruno. "Yes," said Frederick. "It will be our pleasure."

"And take the baby with you," said the miller. "I would hate for him to get lonely." He laughed heartily and Opal whimpered. I gritted my teeth. This would not be helpful. Bruno untied me and I hoisted the baby's basket in my arms.

When we were outside, Frederick and Bruno hovered next to me as I relieved myself by a tree. "I don't need your help!"

"It's for your safety," said Frederick. "We wouldn't want you to get eaten by trolls."

Trolls. A little egg cracked in my brain. I knew some trolls. Trolls that could smell magic and hoarded it and guarded a poison apple tree, a stiltskin.

"No," I said. "That would be awful."

The egg cracked all the way open, and suddenly my idea emerged. It was a little crazy, and dangerous perhaps, but I had to do something.

"You know," I said, considering my words carefully. "There are other things out there besides trolls. Just beyond the gates, a little ways in The Eastern Woods, I've actually hidden a stash of gold."

"Gold?" Bruno licked his lips as if I'd just said "lamb chops."

"Gold," I said. "I can't carry it all on my own. But if you help me, I'll split it with you."

Their eyes glittered. Bruno nodded, but Frederick pulled him back. "How do we know you're not tricking us, just so you can run away?"

I pointed to the castle. "Red's still in there. I wouldn't run away. And, besides, it's dangerous in those woods. There might be wolves or witches or trolls out there. I just thought I might have a better chance if you were with me, because you're soldiers now. I could wait until I'm done with your father, but then he might find out about it and want the gold for himself."

Frederick whispered something in Bruno's ear, and a greedy grin spread across his face. "We'll help you," they said at the same time.

"But we get most of it," said Frederick. "There's two of us and one of you, and what do you need with gold?"

"I don't need much," I said.

Frederick pushed me to start moving. "You'll get as much as you're worth, Butt."

# CHAPTER THIRTY

## The Stiltskin

Because Frederick and Bruno were soldiers and something like nobility, they were able to get a carriage with horses from the stables.

"Better if we're quick," said Frederick. "I'll send a message to Father and tell him you're having a hard time." Bruno snorted. Frederick found a gnome and gave him the message, and then we left.

When I had Nothing with me, the journey to the trolls' forest had taken half a day, he was so slow, but with the carriage, we were there within half an hour. Bruno whipped the horses so they went faster and we bounced along the road.

Archie woke with the whips and the roar of the carriage and started to wail. I tried to rock him and shush him, but he was awkward in my arms and he only cried louder.

"Where is this place?" Bruno yelled over the baby's

wails. "You said it was just beyond the gates." Bruno looked through the trees as if a wolf might jump out from them at any moment.

"Slow down. Just a bit farther." We came to the bend in the road that I recognized.

"Stop," I told him, and Archie quieted as the carriage became still. We stepped down, and I walked off the road. "Through here," I said, pointing into the blackness of the trees. Frederick and Bruno halted at the edge of the road.

"In *there?*" they asked at the same time. Frederick's voice cracked.

"I *had* to hide the gold in a place where no one else would find it." I walked into the trees. A few moments later, I heard their footsteps behind me. We walked slowly and quietly until we came to the apple tree. Its branches bowed, heavy with the weight of poisoned fruit. I really hoped Bork was still trying to catch a pet, even though he already had Nothing.

Gently, I sat the baby down on the ground. "Wait here," I told them, and approached the tree. There was very little light to see by, but I searched around the tree until I saw it. The snare. Very carefully, I placed my foot into the trap.

*SNAP!*

*Schwip!*

*Schlunk!*

The rope yanked me off the ground, and I screamed louder than necessary, to attract the trolls. Frederick's and Bruno's jaws dropped. A few moments later, rustling came from the brush behind me and the first of the trolls appeared, ugly and smelly as ever. "Trolls!" I shouted. "Help! Trolls! Trolls! Help me!"

Frederick and Bruno squealed and ran, flailing their arms. They didn't even pause to pick up their baby nephew. They bolted through the trees toward the carriage. I barely heard the crack of the whip or the horses' hooves above their screams. In a few moments, the noise faded.

"What's this?" said one of the trolls. "Didn't you learn anything from last time?"

"Hello, Bork."

Archie began crying.

"And you brought extra," said Bork. "Well, we can always use a side dish."

"Oh, you don't want that," I said. "Far too bitter. Do you have any sludge?"

"We always have sludge." And he cut me down.

The first part of the plan had worked—I was out of the castle, and Frederick and Bruno were gone—but that was the easy part. Now I had to find a stiltskin before it was too late. Something told me I was in the right place.

I was greeted with many snorts and snarls from the trolls. Slop now had a wolf pelt on his head, instead of his deer antlers. "How did you get that?" I asked.

"He ate the apples," said Slop.

"Wolves don't eat apples," Bork corrected. "He died of starvation. Didn't even have any meat on his bones."

"Because them apples ate it all up with their poison."

Slop pushed down the wolf head so its teeth were hanging over his eyes. Then he sniffed me. "You still reek of magic."

I wanted to tell him he reeked of troll, but I didn't.

Mard hugged me when she saw me, which was comforting despite the smell. "What is this?" she said, pointing to Archie in the basket.

"That's . . . Archie," I said without explanation.

"He's horribly clean, and so are you." Mard took Archie from my arms, and Gorp and Grot tackled me to the ground and smeared mud in my clothes. As I stood up, a fat donkey came trotting toward me.

"Nothing!" He brayed and pushed me with his head right back down in the mud.

"We named him Horace," said Grot. "He likes to eat worms."

I laughed. Nothing's name is Horace and he likes to eat worms. Well, he looked happy. Maybe having a real name made him a better donkey.

Mard pushed a cup of sludge into my hands. "You need fattening," she said. "You grew." Then she dipped her fingers in the sludge and fed some to Archie. I thought for sure he would start crying, but he didn't. He slurped and gurgled. The young prince had a taste for worms. "This will make him a strong boy," said Mard.

"Why have you come back?" asked Bork. "And who were those boys?"

"Those were the queen's brothers."

"Can they make gold from straw too?" Bork asked. "They didn't look too smart."

"They can't make gold. Neither can the queen." I took a deep breath. "I can, though."

All the slurping and grunting and snorting stopped, and the trolls stared at me. So I told them my story. All of it. The spinning, my mother, my name, and how I had come to gain Archie.

"No wonder you reek of magic," said Slop. "You were *born* in the stuff!

"Why can't you give him back if you don't want him?" Slop asked.

"Because she promised him in exchange for the gold, so I have to take him. That's part of the magic."

"Why would she promise her baby?" asked Gorp.

"I don't know. Humans do a lot of things that make no sense. . . ."

The trolls grunted in agreement and raised their cups.

Archie started to cry, and Mard bounced and rocked him. "Too clean, poor thing." She took handfuls of mud and slathered it on his face so he looked like a piglet in a mud puddle. I thought for sure he'd go into hysterics, but instead he stopped crying and drifted off in Mard's arms as she rocked him. Watching this, I felt a pang in my chest. A baby should have a mother and a mother should have her baby. That is, if destiny works out the way it's supposed to. I needed to find a way to give Archie back to Opal. That's why I had come here.

"I have something to show you," said Bork.

"What is it?"

"Something I discovered a little while ago. Let's go to the tree."

We took a torch through the trees until we came to the clearing with the apple tree, standing so still and perfect in the dark. Bork reached up and picked an apple and held it to the light of his torch.

"This tree grew from the seeds of a poisoned apple, you know, so I've never tried one, but a few weeks ago I saw a strange thing. A family of raccoons came out in the middle of the night and started eating those apples. I watched them, followed them to their den, and they didn't die. They didn't even seem sick. So I thought maybe those apples aren't poisonous for raccoons. But I kept watching the tree and a week later I saw some squirrels gnawing at the apples, and they didn't get sick either. So you know what else I thought? Maybe those apples aren't really poisonous at all. Maybe poison doesn't have to grow from poison. Not always. This tree, I think just maybe it grew the way it wanted to grow. Those seeds, they were stronger than the magic."

Without warning, Bork took a bite of the apple.

I snatched it and threw it away. "What are you doing?"

He chewed and swallowed, and we waited. My heart pounded as I thought that any moment Bork was going to drop dead. He smacked his lips and grimaced. Surely the poison was sinking in now. "Not as good as sludge," he said. "Well, I just thought that might be useful to you. You can think about it."

"Think about what?"

"The things you know that you don't know you know. You're not so bright compared to a troll, but you're a crumb smarter than most humans."

"Thank you," I said. "But I'm not sure I understand."

"You humans always talk about magic and destiny like it's the most powerful thing in the world. Like it controls you."

"Doesn't it?"

"I guess it does if you want it to. Maybe it does other humans, but *you*, Rump? You were *born* with *magic*. I can smell it stronger on you than on any magical object I've ever found, even stronger than this tree."

"But that's the problem!" I said. "It's the magic that's caused all this trouble, just like all those things in your hoard cause trouble. I can't do anything about it!"

"It's the *people* who cause the trouble, Rump. Not the magic itself. If you're so full of magic, why should you be helpless?"

"I don't know." I felt dizzy with confusion.

Bork handed me the torch. "Think about it. It's not so hard." He walked back into the trees.

Everything was cold and quiet now, except for the crackle of the torch. I stared at the apple tree. I still couldn't believe Bork ate one. Maybe that poison didn't work on trolls. Maybe it only worked on princesses. Or maybe Bork was right. *Those seeds really were stronger than the magic.*

I am not a tree. I was born with a name and that name is my destiny. Rumpel has me wrapped and trapped. It controls me. My destiny controls me.

But then a new question entered my mind.

What is destiny?

I knew that everyone had one, just as they had a name. And they were one and the same. Just as no person chooses their own name, no person chooses their own destiny. It isn't up to them. But what if that wasn't so? If Red's granny said that I must *find* my destiny, doesn't that mean I have some say in where to look?

Maybe destiny isn't something that just happens. Maybe destiny is something you *do*. Maybe destiny is like a seed and it *grows*. I wasn't powerless. Even with my name, even with all the snares and tangles, I could do things, like spin straw into gold, and make terrible mistakes that ended up with girls being carried to their doom and promising me their firstborn child. That was all part of my destiny.

My name is Rumpel.

My name means I am bound, but I can grow more powerful than those bindings.

I am more than the name I have always known.

Deep inside I have a power that no one can take away from me. A deep magic more powerful than any magic placed upon me. A magic that I was born with, that grew inside me, deep in my bones.

A stiltskin.

I am Rumpel. I am a stiltskin.

Rumpel.

Stiltskin.

I pictured my mother, holding me in her arms, dying, ready to give me a name, a name that would overpower all the magic that had trapped her. She whispered it to me. It was a name that would make me everything I am. No one else had ever heard it but me. My name is my destiny. My name is my power.

Rumpel. Stiltskin.

I heard Mother's whisper reaching across years and mountains and valleys.

Rumpel. Stiltskin.

Rumpelstiltskin.

The name, *my* name, shook in my chest. It traveled through my brain and down my arms and fingertips to my legs and toes. The sound of it echoed so loud inside of me I felt I would burst.

I made a rhyme then and there. A rhyme full of powerful words to release into the black night.

> *Tomorrow I'm free*
> *Today I'm alive*
> *The curses and tangles no longer survive*
> *From deep within, the wisdom came*
> *That Rumpelstiltskin is my name!*

*I* was a stiltskin. And that power was greater than the rumpel. I felt it now, all inside of me, as if just saying my name out loud had unleashed a force and it was wrapping around the tangles, ready to rip them apart.

I picked an apple from the tree and took a bite, sweet juice filling my mouth. "I am more powerful than a tree!" I shouted into the night air, and I laughed and danced.

A flickering shadow caught my eye and I froze mid-laugh. Frederick stepped from behind a tree into the clearing, his arms trembling as he held up a bow and arrow.

"Don't move," he said. "Come out, Bruno." He kicked at his brother, who squealed and slid out from behind another tree holding a spear tight to his chest. He was white as the moon and shaking so hard it was as if some outside force were throttling him.

"Don't move," Frederick said again, pointing his bow and arrow at me. "You have to come back with us. You still have to spin all that gold, or your friend is going to get hurt. *You're* going to get hurt." Frederick took a step forward. Bruno took a step back and whimpered, mumbling, "Trolls, filthy trolls, cursed trolls."

I dropped my apple. I wasn't afraid of Frederick or Bruno anymore. They looked pathetic and small, quivering with their weapons. I was amazed that I had ever been afraid of them, had ever allowed them to bully me. But I also realized I wasn't free yet. I had found my name. I still felt it inside me. The magic of my stiltskin was still rushing through my arms and legs and my brain, making me big and powerful. But the rumpel had yet to be untangled. Red was still trapped in the castle. There was still the miller to face. I still had Archie with me. And no one could untangle it all but me.

# CHAPTER THIRTY-ONE

## Third Day's the Charm

Archie slept soundly in the basket, caked in mud and swaddled tightly in blankets. He needed to go back to his mother, and he would. I knew that now. Nothing was binding me anymore, not the miller or the gold or a rumpel. I knew I could set everything right, and I started to spin the final stages of my plan.

"Bet you thought you were being clever," said Frederick. He was still pointing his arrow at me as we walked, and he trembled less and less the farther we got from the trolls. We had to walk because apparently the horses got spooked when Frederick and Bruno ran screaming, and the carriage took off without them. "Bet you thought you could outsmart us," Frederick continued. "Are you friends with the trolls, then? Father always said you were unnatural, a demon. Maybe you're a demon troll."

Bruno whimpered and stepped farther away from me. He looked as if he thought I would turn into a troll and eat him.

"Trolls are actually quite nice," I said. "Much nicer than you."

"Ha!" scoffed Frederick. "You *are* a little demon!"

The sky was lightening, and we were almost back to the castle. As we traveled, I scanned the sides of the road for what I needed. With all the gold in the castle, the pixies were naturally drawn to this place. There had to be nests everywhere. I looked carefully between rocks and in the nooks of trees. There! I could see one resting just inside a hollow tree.

"Where are you going?" asked Frederick as I fearlessly moved off the road.

"Nature calls again."

"Get back here or I'll shoot you!"

"Now, Frederick, I don't think I'll be able to spin gold very well if you do that." I smiled back at him, enjoying his furious expression. Bruno pranced back and forth like he might wet himself.

When I reached the tree, I gingerly removed the pixie nest and placed it in the side of Archie's basket. The ground was still frozen, so I knew the pixies would be sleeping. I found two more in some shrubs, and another sticking out from a shallow crevice between the roots of a tree. That one was shiny. I looked closer, and to my surprise and delight, the nest was woven with fine strands of gold. So King Barf hadn't been able to keep all his gold safe.

"All right, come out now, or I'm going to come in there after you!" shouted Frederick.

Quickly, I tucked Archie's blankets around the nests to hide them. Then I took off my coat and clawed into the hard ground for dirt and piled it up in my coat. Archie slept soundly through it all; mothers all over The Kingdom might like to know the trolls' recipe for sludge.

Last, I reached into my satchel and pulled out Opal's necklace and ring. I tucked them in Archie's blankets in hopes that they would soon be returned to Opal: their true owner.

"Butt!" shouted Frederick. "If you're not back here in ten seconds, I'll come in there and drag you out by your ears!" He sounded serious now. I rolled up my coat and tucked it beneath my arm.

"You're a strange little demon," said Frederick as I came out from the brush. "What do you want with a baby, anyway?"

I just smiled, because I knew they wouldn't believe even a tiny speck of my story.

As we reached the castle, the sun rose fully in the sky, its rays bursting all around the towers and turrets. I took deep breaths of the cold morning air. This was it. It was time to face all my tangles and traps.

As we walked through the gates, I felt one of the pixie nests shift.

"That was very foolish," said the miller. "Your friend was afraid you had left her to die." Red was on the floor, still bound and gagged, and she had a large, fresh welt on her cheek. The miller had hit her again!

"My baby!" cried Opal. "Give him to me!"

The miller shoved Opal back as she rushed forward. "He's not your baby anymore, you silly girl! You can have another!" Opal collapsed on the floor, sobbing. Bruno knelt down next to her and patted her on the back.

"Now spin the gold, boy," said the miller.

"No," I said shakily. For all the bravery I had felt in the presence of Frederick and Bruno, the miller still frightened me.

"What?" asked the miller, his voice soft and dangerous.

Red looked at me, her eyes wide with confusion.

A faint hum came from the nests in the basket. No one else seemed to notice, but to me it was shrill. I was shaking. The miller's face was nearly purple. He clenched and unclenched his fists. All the power I had felt just hours before had abandoned me. My words felt small and weak.

"I won't spin," I whispered.

Oswald stepped close to me, his belly pressed against Archie's basket and the nests. The humming grew louder. Archie began to squirm, and he chirped like a small bird, or was it the pixies chirping? Not much time . . .

"We made a bargain, boy. What do you think will happen to your little friend if you don't keep your bargain?"

Bargains, bargains . . . the *bargain*! I saw it now. "You have not kept your bargain either," I said.

"What?" snarled Oswald. "Your friend is still alive! I could have—"

"That is not what you promised. You promised me my friend unharmed. Clearly, you have broken your promise, and so there is no bargain."

The miller's face turned a deeper red than his cherry tomato tunic. He clawed at the pile of gold next to him as though he thought to strangle me with it, but then he shouted with alarm when he realized that he could not pick it up. Just as with Opal before, the magic would not let the miller have the gold.

"No bargain, no gold," I said with a smile.

"Why, you—" The miller lunged at me.

"I have something to say," said Opal.

"Not now, girl." The miller grabbed my ear and twisted.

"No! I am the queen!" Opal was standing up now with Frederick and Bruno behind her. "You don't order me anymore! I am queen."

The miller released me, shoving me so hard I crumpled to the floor, barely catching Archie in the basket. One nest plopped to the floor, and a pixie emerged from it sleepily. He fluttered to my hand.

"You," said Opal, pointing a trembling finger at me. "You told me if I guessed your name in three days, you would give me back my child."

I stared at Opal. She wanted to play guessing games now?

"I don't—"

"No!" she screamed. "You promised and I'm going to tell you your name, and then you will give me back my baby."

She paced before me. Everyone was silent, waiting to see what she would do. "Is your name Robert? No. Dan? No. It's not Balthasar or Nebuchadnezzar or Spindleshanks or Cruikshanks. I know what your name is." She whirled on me, full of gleeful triumph. "Is your name *Rumpelstiltskin?*" She tilted her head back and laughed maniacally. Behind her Frederick and Bruno grinned, like they had some delicious secret. They must have heard me say my name by the apple tree.

Rumpelstiltskin. Yes. That was my name. I had almost forgotten. For just a moment, I had still been Rump, small and helpless. But I wasn't small anymore. I wasn't stupid. I wasn't weak. I was tangled in a million ways, but I was strong and smart. I was a stiltskin. I pulled myself up off the floor and the pixie flitted away.

"Now give me back my baby!" Opal shouted. She ran to the basket and snatched Archie. Another nest rolled to the floor.

Opal screamed when she looked at Archie, seeing the mud caked on his face. "What have you done to him, you demon!" She rushed at me, claws outstretched, teeth bared like a wild beast.

Now was the time. It all happened in a moment, but somehow my brain sped up so that everything around me slowed down. All the things I knew now—my name, my destiny, my power—they all converged and made me strong, my mind clear so I could do what I had to do.

*Watch your step.*

"Yes, yes, yes!" I shouted. "You guessed right! My name is Rumpelstiltskin!" I stomped my foot on a pixie nest, and a hiss like a boiling kettle filled the air. I stomped on another nest and another. The floorboards beneath me raised and cracked. Everyone stood frozen, staring at me. The buzz rose to shrieks, and then the room exploded with pixies.

Opal screamed and hovered over her baby while the miller and his sons flailed their arms and legs. I shook out my coat and dumped dirt all over Red and myself just as the pixies pelted toward us. They swerved around the cloud of dirt and aimed instead for the miller and his sons.

I yanked Red to her feet and stomped again on the cracked and splintered wood that Opal had weakened with her incessant rocking. I kept on stomping until the floorboards groaned. Just before the floor collapsed, I threw the last nest at the spinning wheel. The pixies exploded all over the gold as Red and I plummeted through the floor.

We landed in a pile of potatoes—mashed potatoes now—in the castle kitchen.

Martha screamed, hovering above us with a long knife.

"Oh!" she exclaimed when she saw my face. "It's you, Robert." She lowered her knife.

I stood up and brushed myself off. "Hello, Martha. Could I borrow that?" I took the knife in her hand and cut the ropes from Red's wrists and ankles. She pulled off her gag and gasped for breath.

Martha looked from the ceiling down to Red and me. The shouts and screams echoed above us. The pixies must be going nuts with all that gold. "Robert, what in the world . . ."

"My name isn't really Robert," I said to Martha. "It's Rumpelstiltskin."

"Rump . . . what?" said Martha.

"Rumpelstiltskin. Isn't that a wonderful name? I'll tell you my whole story someday. It's a really good one. But now isn't the best time. May we . . . ?" I nodded in the direction of the kitchen door. Martha simply gaped. She looked from me back up to where shrieks and screams and stomps rattled the ceiling. I took Red's hand and walked toward the door.

"Wait!" said Martha. "Take some pies!"

We grabbed the food, thanked Martha, and then ran for it.

# CHAPTER THIRTY-TWO

## From Small Things

While everyone else's attention was on the commotion above, we made a hasty dash through the gates. The pixies had started throwing skeins of gold out the windows, and men and women were scrambling about to pick them up, but of course they couldn't. As soon as it hit the ground, the gold became like stones melded into the earth. We heard shouts as people tried to pry up the gold and then got attacked by pixies. I guess the pixies had claimed this gold as their own. They would have gold nests all over the castle now.

By the time we reached the base of The Mountain, the day was nearly gone. Red and I didn't speak much as we traveled. We were cold and dirty and exhausted, but at least we were full from the pies Martha had given us.

As we slowly climbed The Mountain, Red kept glancing

back toward the castle, her face knit into something like worry.

"They won't come after us," I said. "I think they're a little busy."

"No, it isn't that. I just . . . Do you think they'll be all right?"

I had to laugh. Red, concerned? And about the miller, no less! "They'll be fine, once the swelling goes down."

Then we both laughed, tears streaking our muddy faces.

"How did you do that?" she asked. "How did you . . . just *do* all that?"

I smiled. "A good name can do a lot for you."

I told Red everything that had happened when Frederick and Bruno took me outside, all about my name, and how I knew what it was and my plan to get away.

"Rumpelstiltskin," she said slowly. "That's crazy. You're trapped and tangled, but then you're really powerfully magical."

"Who isn't?"

She patted me on the head. "You're a lot smarter than you look."

Well, that's friendship.

"And you really *are* taller than me," she said, holding her hand up to my head. "Not that it's saying much," she finished, punching me in the arm.

That's friendship too.

We reached the edge of The Village just as the sun was going down, casting a sparkling pink glow all over the snow. Gran's cottage was dark and empty and cold. It looked so lonely.

"You can come to my house. Mother wouldn't mind. She'll probably want to thank you for, you know, saving my life."

"Maybe in a little while."

Red nodded. She understood. After everything, I needed some time alone.

I walked around The Village, glancing through candle-lit windows where families ate their suppers or children were snuggling in their beds.

I walked past the mill, now abandoned and silent. I wondered who would be the miller now. Surely no one as greedy as Oswald.

I walked through the mines, where tools were abandoned and the pans full of mud suggested that the villagers still were not finding much gold.

I walked just inside The Woods and felt the mysteries there. One day I would go back to Red's granny and thank her.

Nothing had changed about The Mountain or The Village, but it all looked different to me, I guess because I had changed.

When I came back to the cottage, I noticed something that really *was* different. There was a hardy little sapling growing in the snow in front of the cottage. My seed! Red must have come and watered it, or maybe even her granny. *Big things can grow from small ones.* What would it grow to be? I hoped a giant apple tree.

Inside the cottage, I found my mother's spinning wheel in front of the fireplace, old and scratched. It had caused so much trouble, but it was still beautiful to me, because it was hers. Because now I knew the destiny she had wished for me. I brushed my hands over the wood and spun the wheel, its *whir* ringing like music. I still had my mother's bobbin in my satchel. I took it out and placed it on the wheel. I gathered a few bits of straw from the floor and held them tight in my hand.

Red once told me that magic was inside of me. She was right. But Ida had said that magic was everywhere—in the sky, in the air, in the sun. She was right, too. The magic was inside me and outside me, in everyone and everything. And everything had its own unique kind of magic. It was in trees and trolls, squirrels and rabbits, mountains and rivers and rocks. It was in my feet and fingers and in my heart. I could feel it now as I began to spin.

*Straw is straw*, I thought. The straw snapped and sputtered through the wheel. It floated in the air, glittering in the moonlight like bits of gold dust. *Like* gold, but not gold. Beautiful. Gran would have loved it, and so would Mother. I could almost feel them with me. And that's its own kind of magic—to feel that people who are gone are still here.

# EPILOGUE

## Your Destiny Is Your Name

For days and weeks, I woke with my name singing in my ears. It was a beautiful sound, music unlike any in the world. It made me wish that everything could have such a name. Not just people, but animals and villages, and roads and kingdoms, even mountains.

When spring arrived, Red and I climbed as high up on The Mountain as we could, until we could see all The Village and the roads, The Kingdom, and far away, just the faint glimpse of Yonder and Beyond. My whole journey was laid out before me. I imagined I could see the trolls in The Eastern Woods, slurping sludge and maybe eating apples. I saw my aunts in Yonder, spinning their magic, Ida making rhymes and cake. Someday I would visit them again and spin and weave with their magic. And instead of tying me up in knots, the magic would bring us together. But for now I was home, back where it all began. And I had one last task to fulfill.

"I'm going to give this mountain a name," I said.

"Why?" asked Red. "It doesn't need a destiny like we do."

"Yes, it does," I said. "Everything in the world should have a destiny. And come together and get all intertwined and tangled with our own destinies."

"Sounds like trouble," said Red.

I smiled. "It probably is. But what is destiny without a little trouble?"

And right then and there, I stood up and hollered the name of my mountain. The name soared into the sky and clouds. I could feel the magic of it spreading over the mountain, sinking into the ground, and running right up through my feet, bursting with power and fateful glory.

A name is a powerful thing.

# THE END

# AUTHOR'S NOTE

"What's in a name? That which we call a rose by any other name would smell as sweet." Shakespeare immortalized these words in his tragic play *Romeo and Juliet*. The words sound true, yet I also agree with my childhood heroine Anne Shirley when she said, "I don't believe a rose *would* be as nice if it was called a thistle or a skunk cabbage."

As I interact with other people, sometimes I can't help but think their names reflect their looks and behavior with such exactness. Did their parents intuitively know that was the name for them, or did the name have a role in shaping their behavior and self-perception? There are many studies and theories to support the notion that our names have a significant bearing on our development and sense of identity, and perhaps even our confusion about identity.

As a child, I was terribly shy about my name, and to this day, whenever I introduce myself, people always ask me to repeat it, and sometimes spell it. Then they say the inevitable, "That's . . . different." And so I felt different. Every year when school started, I kept hoping there would be another Liesl in the class. There were always two or three Ashleys or Jennifers—sometimes even four—but no Liesls. And then of course there were the rhyming taunts of "Liesl the Weasel" or "Liesl Diesel" (a torture I'm sure many kids can relate to). Perhaps the saddest thing about my name was that I could never find it on any of those personalized pencils and key chains in gift shops. I searched all the time, and kept hoping I would find my name between "Leslie" and "Lisa," but to no avail. There was no question I was different, but this made me feel like I wasn't even real.

I have long thought names were significant, and if ever there was a tale that showed their importance, it is "Rumpelstiltskin." And yet, for the crucial role Rumpelstiltskin and his name play in the story, we know so little about him in the traditional tale. We know nothing of where he comes from, what his name means, how he gained the power to spin straw into gold, or why on earth he would want someone's firstborn child.

So as I set out to tell the tale behind the fairy tale of "Rumpelstiltskin," I imagined a world where names were directly tied to a person's destiny. A name would determine not only your personality, but your future. I wanted *Rump* to go beyond the tale that inspired it, just as Rump learns to move beyond the name he was born with, and the assumptions people make because of it.

And so Rump's adventures began. The story went through many changes along the way, but the heart of it has always remained the same. *Rump* was my way of answering that age-old question, "What's in a name?" To all those with common names, rare names, beautiful names, strange and exotic names, or names they wish they could change: Names are powerful and so is destiny, but a person's will is more powerful than both put together.

# ACKNOWLEDGMENTS

Many thanks to my editor, Katherine Harrison, for not only her sharp critical eye but also for nurturing my story with childlike love and enthusiasm.

To my agent, Michelle Andelman, who was the first stranger to fall in love with my work and has been by my side every step of the way.

To my critique partners—Kate Coursey, Ali Cross, Krista Van Dolzer, Jennifer Jensen, and Jenilyn Tolley. You are all ferociously talented and kind.

To my mother, who worked so hard to give me opportunities, and to my father, who believed I had no limits. And I must mention all seven of my siblings—Adria, Carrie, Paul, Patrick, Chad, Caitlin, and Marisa.

Sometimes you were my best friends and other times my worst enemies, but thanks for all the material!

To my children, Whitney, Ty, and Topher, who thought it was supercool to let Mom go work on her book. (Probably because you got away with all sorts of things with Dad in charge, like eating marshmallows for dinner.)

And more thanks than I can ever express to my husband, Scott, without whom this book would certainly never have come about. You make life endlessly fun and adventurous.

**A**ll the tales say that Snow White
was a perfect little princess.
They say the seven dwarves were
sneezy and dopey and grumpy.
But did anyone ever ask the dwarves for
*their* side of the story?

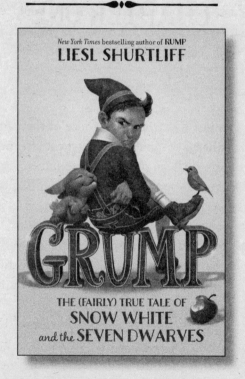

## READ ON FOR A SNEAK PEEK!

# CHAPTER ONE

## Odd Little Dwarfling

I was born just feet from the surface of the earth, completely unheard of for a dwarf, but it couldn't be helped. Most dwarves are born deep underground, at least a mile below The Surface, preferably in a cavern filled with crystals and gems: diamonds for strength, emeralds for wisdom, and sapphires for truth.

Mothers and fathers try to feed their dwarflings as many healthy powerful gems as they can within a few hours of birth, to give them the best chance in life. But I was fed none.

My parents had been traveling downward the day I was born. Mother could feel me turning hard inside her belly, a sign that the time was drawing near. She wanted the very best for me. She wanted to be as deep in the earth as possible, in the birthing caverns, with their rich deposits of nutritious crystals and gems. But as my parents traveled downward, before they had even descended below the main caverns, there was a sudden collapse in one of the tunnels. The rocks nearly crushed my mother, and me with her. My father was able to get us out of the way just in time.

Unfortunately, the collapse had blocked the tunnel, so we had to go up to find another way down. The strain of the climb was too much for my poor mother.

"Rubald!" she cried, clutching her belly. "It's time!"

And there was no time to waste. A dwarfling can stay inside its mother's belly for a solid decade or more, but when we're ready to come out, we come fast.

And so I was born in a cavern mere feet below the earth's surface, where roots dangled from the ceiling, water trickled down the walls, and the only available food was a salty gruel called *strolg*, made out of common rocks and minerals. Mother was devastated.

"My poor little dwarfling!" she cooed as she spooned the strolg into my mouth, then fed me a few pebbles to satisfy my need to bite and crunch. "What kind of life will he have, Rubald?"

"A fine life, Rumelda," said my father, ever the optimist. "A happy life."

"And what will we call him?"

My parents both looked at their surroundings. Dwarves were usually named with some regard to the gems and crystals within the cavern in which they were born, but there were no diamonds or sapphires in that cavern. Not even quartz or marble. Just plain rocks and roots.

Father brushed his hands over the rough walls, studying the layers of dirt and minerals. "Borlen," he said with wonder.

Borlen was a mineral found only near The Surface. It was not so common in our colony but useful when it could be found. It was too bitter to eat, but potters liked it because it made their clay more malleable without weakening it. Borlen could also serve as a warning. A mining crew knew by the sight of it that they were digging dangerously close to The Surface. Most dwarves would rather not find any.

"We'll call him Borlen," said Father.

"You don't think that name will make him seem a bit . . . odd?" Mother asked.

"No, it's special," said Father. "He'll be one of a kind, our dwarfling. We'll get him deep into the earth as soon as possible and feed him all the best crystals and gems. But wait!" My father pulled something from his pocket and held it out to my mother. "I almost forgot. I've been saving this from the moment I knew we had a dwarfling on the way."

Mother gasped. "A ruby!"

Rubies were rare and particularly powerful gems. They could ward off evil, enhance powers, and even lengthen lives. Emegert of Tunnel 588 was said to have found a large deposit of rubies, and he lived for ten thousand years. Two thousand years was considered a good long life for a dwarf.

Mother took the ruby from my father and dropped it onto my tongue. I crunched on the gem, gave a little belch, and fell asleep.

The very next day, my parents tried to move me to deeper caverns, but as soon as they started to carry me downward, I began to cry. The deeper we went, the louder I wailed, until my eyes leaked tears of dust, a sign of deep distress and discomfort from any dwarf.

"Oh dear," said Mother. "Rubald, I think our dwarfling is afraid of depths!"

"Nonsense," said Father. "He only needs to adjust."

But I did not adjust. I cried for hours on end. My parents tried everything to console me. They fed me amber, amethysts, and blue-laced agate. They bathed me in crushed rose quartz and hung peridot above my cradle, all to no avail. And so, distraught from my endless wails, and desperate to try anything, my parents took me back to the cavern near The Surface where I was born.

I stopped crying.

"Oh dear," said Mother.

"How odd," said Father.

And after that, my parents were obliged to make my unfortunate birthing cavern our home, hoping my fear of depths would subside eventually. But it didn't. It only got worse.

**R**ed is not afraid of the big bad wolf.
She's not afraid of witches or pixies
or deep, dark caves,
or even enchanted beasts.
No, Red is not afraid of anything, except *magic*.
And there's magic at every turn in this tale!

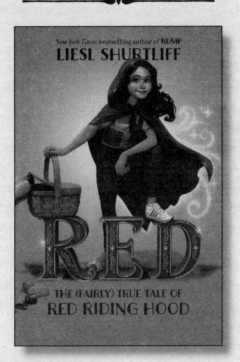

# READ ON FOR A SNEAK PEEK!

When I was six, I had a friend named Gertie. We were only allowed to play at her house with constant supervision from her mother, Helga. Helga was always worried. She worried Gertie would fall in a well or off a cliff. She worried Gertie would choke on her morning mush. She worried trolls would come in the night and carry Gertie away for their supper. This worrying became problematic when I wanted to take Gertie into The Woods to play.

"Mother says I'll be eaten by wolves," Gertie said.

"You won't," I said. "I've never been eaten by wolves, and I play in The Woods all the time."

"Don't you ever get lost? Mother is always afraid I'll lose my way."

"I'm never lost. I have a magic path." Gertie's eyes got as big as apples. Magic was rare, and my path was something special. It only appeared when I wanted it to, and it led me wherever I wanted to go in The Woods. Surely this would entice Gertie to come with me, but it didn't. She stepped away from me. Her eyes grew wary.

"Mother says magic is dangerous."

"My path isn't dangerous," I said with indignation. "Granny made it to keep me safe. She made it grow right out of the ground after a bear attacked me and I almost died." I thought this would impress her. The possibility of death was always exciting, and being able to defy it with magic was even better.

"Mother says your granny is a witch," said Gertie.

Of course Granny was a witch. I knew that, but Gertie said it like it was a bad thing. Desperation took hold of me. I *really* wanted to play with Gertie in The Woods. So I did the only sensible thing I could think of. I cast the Worrywart Spell on Gertie's mother.

### Worrywart Spell
*Worry's a wart upon your chin*
*It spreads and grows from deep within*
*Make the wart shrink day by day*
*Send your worries far away*

Unfortunately, the spell did nothing to cure Helga's worries. Instead, she grew a wart on her chin. The wart grew steadily bigger, day by day, until Granny was summoned to remedy my mistake. Needless to say, I wasn't allowed to play with Gertie anymore—or anyone else—for, in addition to being a worrywart, Helga was also the village gossip. The news spread all over The Mountain.

"She's a witch," Helga told the villagers, "just like her grandmother." She seemed to forget it was Granny who had cured her.

Gertie stopped talking to me, and no one else would even look at me. The magic in me grew hot and sticky. It coated my throat. It stung my eyes. I wished I could swallow it down and make it disappear.

"Don't worry, Red," Granny told me. "We all make mistakes. When I was your age, I tried to summon a rabbit to be my pet, and instead I called a bear to the door!"

"No!" I cried. "How did you survive?"

"The bear was actually quite nice. My sister married him."

"She married a *bear?*"

"Oh, don't be ridiculous. He wasn't really a bear. He was a prince under a spell."

This did nothing to alleviate my concerns. I didn't want to marry a bear *or* a prince.

"All the magic I do is bad," I said.

"Nonsense, child," said Granny. "They're only mistakes. It takes a hundred miles of mistakes before you arrive at your own true magic."

"But what if my mistakes are too big?"

"No such thing, dear," said Granny.

But she was wrong. I went on trying spells and charms and potions, and I went on making mistakes. Big ones. Small ones. Deadly ones.

My last mistake was worse than warts, fire, or roses out the nose.

I was seven years old, and Granny and I were in The

Woods. It was early spring, so the trees were just budding. Granny thought I could help them grow.

### Growing Charm
*Root in the earth*
*Sprout above ground*
*Swell in the sun*
*Spread all around*

"What if I burn down The Woods?" I asked, trembling. Fire seemed to be the only magic I had a knack for.

"Don't be afraid, Red," said Granny. She pointed to a tree branch above us, a large one that dipped low enough that I could see the little branches and buds shooting out of it. "Focus on that branch. Feel its energy and the energy inside you. They are connected. See if you can make its leaves grow. Growing is the best kind of magic."

Yes, I loved it when Granny made things grow. She could grow juicy strawberries and fat pumpkins, spicy herbs and fragrant blossoms. Roses. Granny was particularly good with roses.

I focused on the magic inside me. I felt it swirling in my belly, like a bubbling pot of soup ready to spill over. I felt it flow through my arms and to the edges of my fingertips. Then I let the magic pour out of me and flow toward the tree. The buds on the branch swelled and started to unfurl. Nothing exploded. Nothing caught fire.

"I'm doing it!" I said.

"Good!" said Granny. "Keep going!"

Buds kept swelling, leaves unfurling, until the branch

was full of green and pink. Then the branch itself started to grow. It got thicker and longer.

"Slow it down now," said Granny. "Pull that magic back inside."

But I couldn't. The magic bubbled and spilled out of me faster than I could control it. The branch swelled and extended, too big and heavy for the tree. It sagged and creaked.

Everything happened at once.

The branch snapped. Granny pushed me out of the way. As I tumbled to the ground, so did the branch. There was a scream and a crash. When I looked up, Granny was on the ground, trapped under the branch.

Her eyes were closed and she was still.

"Granny?" I raced to her. I shook her shoulder, but she didn't wake. There was blood on her face, a trickle of red that seeped into the lines on her cheek. My heart pounded in my chest. I tried to pull the branch off her, but it was too big and I was too small.

I ran out of The Woods, tears blurring my vision so I could barely see my path. When I reached home, I burst through the door, sobbing.

"She's dead! I killed her! I killed Granny!"

Papa ran into The Woods. Mama held me in her arms as I curled into a ball and trembled like a sapling in a thunderstorm. I cried and cried. In my mind, I could see Granny, eyes closed, still as stone, and the blood on her face bright red. It was a message.

*You did this, Red. You killed your granny.*

Mama could not calm me.

When Papa returned, he got down low and whispered to me. "She's all right, Red. Just a few scratches and a hurt foot. She's just fine." I started crying anew, flooded with relief and sorrow. She was alive, but still I had hurt her. It was my fault.

Granny's foot never quite healed after that. She had to use a cane, and she hobbled like an old lady—like a witch. I hated to see it, but it reminded me every day of what I had done, what I was. Granny may have been a witch, but she was a good witch. Her magic made things live and grow. My magic made them bleed and die. It didn't matter if this was mile ninety-nine of my hundred miles of mistakes, I couldn't journey one step farther.

I would never do magic again.

You might think you know all about
giants and beanstalks
and that foolish boy who traded
his family's cow for some magic beans.
But you don't know JACK!

**READ ON FOR A SNEAK PEEK!**

> Jack was brisk and of a ready,
> lively wit, so that nobody or
> nothing could worst him.
>
> —*Jack the Giant Killer*

# CHAPTER ONE

## A Sprinkling of Dirt

When I was born, Papa named me after my great-great-great-great-great-great-GREAT-grandfather, who, legend had it, conquered nine giants and married the daughter of a duke. Mama said this was all hogwash. Firstly, there was no such thing as giants. Wouldn't we see such large creatures if they really existed? And secondly, we had no relation to any duke—if we did, we'd be rich and living on a grand estate. Instead, we were poor as dirt and lived in a tiny house on a small farm in a little village. Nothing great or giant about it.

But Papa wasn't concerned with the details. He

believed there was greatness in that name, and if he gave it to me, somehow the greatness would sink into my bones.

"We'll name him Jack," Papa said. "He'll be great."

"If you say so," said Mama. She was a practical woman and not particular with names. All she needed was a word to call me to supper, or deliver a scolding. I got my first scolding before my first supper, just after birth, for as soon as Papa pronounced my name, I sprang a sharp tooth, and bit my mother.

"Ouch!" Mama cried. "You naughty boy!" It was something she would call me more often than Jack.

Papa had the nerve to laugh. "Oh, Alice, he's just a baby. He doesn't know any better."

But Mama believed I *did* know better. To her, that bite was a little omen of what was to come, like a sprinkle before the downpour, a buzz before the sting, or the onset of an itch before you realize you're covered in poison ivy.

Maybe I was born to be great, but great at what?

At five months old, I learned to crawl. I was fast as a cockroach, Papa said. One minute I was by Mama's skirts, and the next I was in the pigsty, rolling around in the muck and slops. Mama said she had to bathe me twice a day just to keep me from turning into a real pig.

I learned to walk before my first year, and by my second I took to climbing. I climbed chairs and tables, the woodpile, trees. Once Mama found me on the roof, and snatched me up before I slid down the chimney into a blazing fire.

"Such a naughty boy," said Mama.

"He's just a boy," said Papa.

But I didn't want to be "just a boy." I wanted to be great.

At night, Papa would tell stories of Grandpa Jack: how he'd chop off giants' heads and steal all their treasure and rescue the innocents. I knew if I was going to be great, I'd have to go on a noble quest and conquer a giant—or nine—just like my seven-greats-grandpa Jack.

There was only one problem. I'd never seen a giant in all my twelve years.

# IT ALL HAPPENED ONCE UPON A TIME....

## READ ALL THE *NEW YORK TIMES* BESTSELLING (FAIRLY) TRUE TALES!

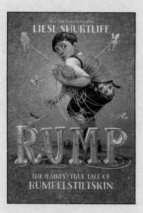

"Lighthearted and inventive."
—Brandon Mull, #1 *New York Times* bestselling author of *Fablehaven*

"Liesl Shurtliff has the uncanny ability to make magical worlds feel utterly real." —Tim Federle, author of *Better Nate Than Ever*

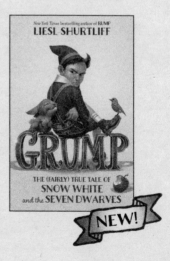

"*Red* is the most wonder-filled fairy tale of them all!" —Chris Grabenstein, *New York Times* bestselling author of *Escape from Mr. Lemoncello's Library*